A S

After yearning for so long to be Sister on Women's Surgical, Staff Nurse Selina Harding is promoted, only to find that now she is expected to solve everyone's problems! Why, she can't even solve her own—particularly when they involve Elliot Richmond, the rudest consultant at Tettington Hospital . . .

A SURGEON CALLS

BY

HAZEL FISHER

MILLS & BOON LIMITED
15–16 BROOK'S MEWS
LONDON W1A 1DR

First published in Great Britain 1985
by Mills & Boon Limited

© Hazel Fisher 1985

Australian copyright 1985
Philippine copyright 1985

ISBN 0 263 75051 5

Set in 11 on 12 pt Linotron Times
03–0585–47,200

Photoset by Rowland Phototypesetting Ltd
Bury St Edmunds, Suffolk
Made and printed in Great Britain by
Richard Clay (The Chaucer Press) Ltd
Bungay, Suffolk.

CHAPTER ONE

WARD THREE at Tettington District General Hospital was quiet at last, and as the ladies settled down again, Staff Nurse Selina Harding gave a sigh of relief.

'What a morning!' Selina's thoughts were put into words by State Enrolled Nurse Mary Baxter. 'First the consultant is late, then we had those two admissions right in the middle of his round! I've never known the like.' Still muttering, SEN Baxter began to ease her ample bulk out of the sisters' office on Women's Surgical.

'Mr Richmond was in one hell of a temper, too,' Selina put in as the SEN was leaving. 'He has some foul moods but this—'

She thought she heard a muffled sound from the nurse, and was about to speak again when the door was flung back and the said Mr Richmond appeared like an avenging angel. Or, in his case, a devil.

Swiftly recovering her poise, Selina rose and smiled at the consultant surgeon. Not by the flicker of an eyelash did she show her consternation. He must have heard her disparaging remark about his moods but she certainly was not about to apologise. Learning how others saw him might teach him some self-control, though she doubted it.

'Have you seen my pen, Staff Nurse? Why didn't you send someone down with it?'

'Pen? Oh, that nice gold one? Have you lost it, sir?' Selina hadn't seen the pen but began a thorough search of the office, simply to humour the man.

'Would I be seeking it if it wasn't lost?' Elliot Richmond's clipped, autocratic tones brought a spark of anger to Selina's blue eyes, but she controlled herself.

'Of course not, sir,' she murmured soothingly. Always agree with consultants even when they were in the wrong. Only ward sisters and above could argue with them. Soon she hoped to be in that position. And then—watch out, Elliot Richmond!

Being tall dark and handsome was Mr Richmond's downfall. If he had been short and fat with thinning grey hair he would have been a much pleasanter person, Selina considered. Of course, then her heart would not go bumpety-bump whenever he appeared, but that would probably be for the best. One glance from those unusual silver-grey eyes and she was lost. It was a good thing he loathed nurses and had a despicable temper. Otherwise she might have found herself falling for him. With his predilection for younger women there was no future for her with Elliot Richmond, and the sooner she came to terms with that fact the better. Mr Richmond would consider that, at twenty-six, the tall and generously-proportioned Selina Harding was over the hill.

'Well?' he barked, startling Selina, whose thoughts had been far from his missing pen. 'You have been searching that drawer for at least five minutes,' he added unfairly, and Selina struggled with her own volatile temper.

'I—I may have picked it up by mistake, Mr Richmond. Sometimes I put—'

'Spare me the explanations!' the surgeon snapped, grey eyes stormy. 'I haven't the time. Send it down when you find it.' This last remark came floating back to her from the middle distance, for Elliot was nearly at the ward doors by then.

Angrily Selina ran trembling fingers through her mousey-coloured curls, almost dislodging her paper cap. That man! She couldn't take much more. Either he disliked big girls or there was something about Selina herself he couldn't stand. Although never exactly friendly towards nurses, even ward sisters, he had an urbane politeness, a rather chilly charm when he chose to exert it—but the politeness and charm seemed to desert him when he met Selina.

What she had done, or failed to do, she didn't know. As far as she was concerned his dislike was groundless. It still hurt, nevertheless. More particularly because she sometimes imagined herself half in love with him. Now, that *was* ridiculous. You could not love someone you didn't even like!

'Shall I send Jane to coffee, Staff?' SEN Baxter, Selina's right-hand woman, bustled in, and Selina nodded weakly.

'Is it that time already? Heavens! It's all Mr Richmond's—' she began bitterly, then checked herself. Golden rule—do not criticise consultants in front of nursing staff. It wasn't professional or polite. Also, the consultant in question might be within earshot! And, for a staff nurse hoping shortly for promotion, it certainly wasn't wise.

There was no time for Selina to take her own break, for the ward round had been late starting due to Elliot having to attend an emergency, and a round always generated a lot of clerical work for ward staff. Never mind, she would enjoy her lunch all the more. Coffee was provided for the doctors after the round, naturally, but Selina never felt sufficiently at ease to drink in front of the aloof Elliot Richmond. He had that effect on most of the nurses. Although his patients adored him, even they were in awe of him. The great sun-tanned god of Tettington DGH!

Ward Three, Women's Surgical, was in Selina's charge at present. The last permanent ward sister had left to start a family. Of course, there were a lot of applicants, but as she had worked on Ward Three for almost a year she felt she had the edge over the outsiders. Having been a staff nurse for four years was a considerable advantage, too.

Unfortunately, another member of the Tettington staff had also applied. If Selina did not get the post she would do her best to work amicably with whoever was appointed, but she could not say the same for the other staff nurse from Tettington. Andrea Forman was full of her own self-importance. At twenty-three she was the youngest applicant and did not stand much chance. Yet she'd trained here, which Selina had not. On an informal visit to the ward Andrea had upset most of the nurses, not to mention the patients. If Selina was made up she had been told unofficially that Andrea would be her staff nurse! Hardly a diplomatic move, and one that would not be to the patients' advantage.

Selina frowned. Problems, problems. As long as the ward got an efficient and kind Sister, that was all that mattered. There would be other promotion opportunities for her in the future. Busy with her thoughts, she was half-way down the ward before she became aware of someone calling her.

'Staff! Staff Nurse!' Pupil Nurse Louise Coleman's anxious face peered at her from the bathroom, and Selina quickened her pace.

'It's Pam, Staff. I mean Miss Hargreaves. She came over faint.'

Selina smiled reassuringly at the first-year nurse. 'Don't worry. I expect the bathroom was too warm.' She caught hold of Pam Hargreaves' hand and squeezed it.

Their young patient gazed up at her. It was almost as if she could see, yet Pam was blind, and had been from birth. At nineteen, she was the same age as Selina's favourite sister, Peta, and for that reason Selina took a particular interest in the girl.

Pam assured Selina that she felt fine. 'It was just the heat. And I am rather hungry,' she added with an impish grin.

Nurse Coleman put in, 'If you were a nurse you wouldn't be looking forward to lunch! We get rotten food. It's all stodge. Chips with everything. Isn't that right, Staff?'

Selina suppressed a smile as she agreed, then helped Nurse Coleman escort Pam back to bed. The little pupil was irrepressible. She showed signs of becoming a good nurse if she could control her reckless tendencies. She had caused more than one accident on the ward, yet the patients loved her. She was always bright and cheery, even at seven in the morning, and Selina envied her sometimes. It seemed years since *she* was a learner with no great cares, no responsibilities.

It was a sign that she was getting old, when learners seemed so much younger than they used to be. She gave a half-sigh, thinking of the empty years ahead. There was Martin, of course, but . . .

The porter was wheeling the lunch-trolley through the doors of the ward as Selina left her patient's bedside. Lunch already, and the office work not yet completed!

Lunch consisted of individual meals on trays. Patients whenever possible were given a choice of menu, albeit a restricted one. Unless they were on a special diet they could order any item on the menu-cards which were sent up daily. It saved nursing time, anyway, and gave the patients something which they could look forward to.

Apart from the two new admissions, Mrs Bolton and Miss Wise, and the lady who had recently undergone a total gastrectomy, Mrs Funnell, none of the patients were very ill or needed to be fed. Selina sent her capable third-year student, Jane Olphin, off to first lunch. Nurse Coleman was deputised to keep an eye on Pam Hargreaves and see that she had everything she needed close at hand.

After the patients had finished their sweet course, Louise Coleman started to push the heavy trolley out of the ward. It would be left just outside the ward for the porters to take down in the lift in due course.

Selina, sitting in her office, tried to keep one eye on Nurse Coleman and the other eye on her work, which wasn't easy. Experience had taught her that Pupil Nurse Coleman needed constant supervision if accidents were to be avoided.

Then the telephone rang, and as Selina leaned over to answer it there was a commotion at the main ward doors, which were only a few feet from the office. The call, from the Path Lab, necessarily claimed all her attention and she had to trust that SEN Baxter would pick up the pieces.

She heard the enrolled nurse's calm, measured tones as she put down the receiver. Mrs Baxter was gently scolding someone, and that someone could only be Louise Coleman.

'But it was Mr Richmond! Really, it wasn't my fault. Not *this* time!' Nurse Coleman was saying as Selina poked her head out of the office.

Her deep blue eyes widened with horror. Mr Richmond was bending down, and she followed the movement. All around him were scattered papers, his diary—and the missing gold pen.

When he had retrieved his property he straightened up, and his accusing gaze rested upon Selina.

'I'm sorry about the accident, sir,' Selina said smoothly before he had a chance to wipe the floor with her. 'I see your pen turned up after all,' she added brightly, and he looked disconcerted, almost guilty she thought—but dismissed the idea as ridiculous.

With what might be described as a 'speaking look' he strode away, leaving a scarlet-faced Louise Coleman to explain to Selina.

'I'm ever so sorry, Staff Nurse. I really didn't see him,' she insisted. 'He wasn't looking where he was going. It was his fault!'

'So it might have been, but there was no need to say so in front of him,' Selina said sharply. 'It wasn't diplomatic. He could very easily complain to the Principal Tutor.'

Nurse Coleman looked suitably frightened at such a possibility and Selina hoped it wouldn't come to that. With Elliot Richmond, one never knew. She felt he would not go out of his way to complain, but if he happened to meet the Principal Tutor during the next hour or so he could well mention the incident. It would not occur to him that such a complaint might be the final straw. There were a lot of black marks against Nurse Coleman's name already. She made a habit of knocking doctors flying in her enthusiastic rushing about the ward, and not all were as tolerant as old Dr Turner, who beamed at all the young nurses, however accident-prone, and called them 'my dear' all the time!

Ward Three was a twenty-six bedded ward, though they had three vacancies at present, which was rare. Elliot Richmond and Guy Johns shared the beds. Selina liked Mr Johns, or Guy, as he allowed her to call him. He had actively encouraged her to apply for the Sister's post on the ward. He and his wife, a former physiotherapist at the hospital, were kind and understanding.

Despite being tall and well-made, Selina felt inadequate at times; had the same feeling of inferiority, the same need for reassurance and comfort that small, delicate women had. They received comfort often without asking for it. Poor Selina did not. For that reason alone, Mr Johns' kindly encouragement was welcomed.

Selina's footsteps echoed in the now quiet corridors as she left the ward, her thoughts half on her wish to feel more secure, half on the patients. For once there was no one very ill for her to worry about. The two admissions had both been acute abdomens and one had already gone down for surgery. The other was being kept under observation. Her symptoms had subsided a little, though she would probably have an exploratory operation, a laparotomy, tomorrow. That would not be Selina's worry, for tomorrow was her day off, the only one this week.

She frowned. A whole day to do as she wished. Plus the following morning, for she was on late duty on the Friday for a change—Guy's round-day. She would miss the round. Miss him, too, but she could not lean on the man for ever. Wasn't she going to become a ward sister? Sisters knew everything and *never* worried. Every patient knew that!

Selina lived in. Or, rather, she lived in the trained nurses' annexe which stood a little way off from the hospital. She occupied the flatlet on the ground floor which overlooked the front drive. It had a pleasant aspect, particularly now at the height of summer.

She let herself into the flatlet and gazed around without enthusiasm. She was tired. No, bone-weary, fatigued. Tired was too inadequate a word for how she felt.

She removed her navy and red hospital cape and hung it up, then stepped thankfully out of her uniform. The white striped dress did nothing to conceal her ample figure. Even when—*if* she became a Sister—she would not be able to wave those white dresses 'bye-bye'. Ward sisters wore the same pattern, though they were allowed a navy tippet to emphasise the difference in rank. The cap was different, too. Instead of trying to perch a plain paper cap on her riot of natural curls, she would have to struggle with a lacy, pill-box shaped concoction. Pretty but useless, and difficult to keep on curly hair.

The flatlet boasted a tiny bathroom, which was something for which she was grateful. Showers might be more hygienic but nothing was as good as a warm bath filled with scented foam. Selina stepped into the lavender-scented water, then slid deeper, closing her eyes in sheer bliss. Oh, for a spare pair of feet, she remembered thinking, then must have dozed off. Next thing she knew, there was a persistent knocking at the door, and the bath-water was quite cold.

For one awful moment she thought she had spent the night in the bath and that someone was calling her to go on duty. Then reason returned, and she hurriedly stepped on to the bathmat and grabbed a gaudily-coloured beach-towel her sister Peta had bought her for her birthday. There might be an urgent phone call. Perhaps her father . . .

Worry lent wings to her feet, and Selina was about to open the door when she realised how little she had on. It might be a male nurse. 'Who is it?' she called, vigorously drying herself while she waited.

'Telephone,' came the muffled reply. It was a man's voice.

'I'm just coming. Thank you!' she called through the door. Hurriedly flinging a dress over her still-damp body, and not bothering with shoes, she unlocked the door and dashed out to the hall.

Then she came to a sudden halt. The great Elliot Richmond was holding the telephone receiver and beckoning to her. She went a fiery red as the surgeon's interested gaze swept over her.

The damp dress was a shade too tight and left little to the imagination. His silver-grey eyes made their leisurely way down to her long legs and bare feet. Selina automatically followed his gaze, and to her horror she saw little rivulets of water rolling off her feet on to the carpet.

'Fascinating,' he murmured, then pressed the telephone into her unwilling hand before striding upstairs.

Numbly, Selina watched his tall, powerful figure, her mind unable to grasp the fact that, for once, Mr Elliot Richmond *had* noticed her. But what a way to attract his attention!

Miserably, she spoke into the telephone. Her father's calm voice came back at her. 'I wondered when you were going to say something. I thought perhaps Elliot had cut out your sharp tongue!'

He chuckled at his own joke, and Selina spluttered. 'Elliot? I didn't know you knew him!'

There was silence at the other end. Then, 'I do know him, yes, but . . . Anyway, you don't want to talk about doctors, do you? You must see and hear plenty of them in your job.'

Selina wanted to scream. Yes, I *do* want to hear about that particular doctor! she longed to yell down the phone. No, I don't see or hear enough of him. Tell me more! Instead, she made a non-committal noise, then promised her father she would lunch with him at home the next day.

When she rang off, she glanced at the big clock on the wall. Almost eleven-thirty! And what was Elliot Richmond doing in the annexe so late at night? More important, which nurse was being honoured with a visit?

Tettington Hospital boasted a staff swimming-pool, paid for over many years by staff subscription, and the following day was so hot that Selina would have liked nothing better than to spend the day by the small pool, letting the sun and water ease away the fatigue, allowing her worries and doubts to evaporate in the warm air. Yet it wasn't often she got home these days. While her father was a widower she'd felt guilty about being away from home, but not now. In his sixtieth year he had remarried, and Selina could not have been happier for him.

Joan had been a widow, and was only a few years younger than Charles Harding, and Selina had taken to the motherly Joan immediately. The wedding had been last September, on her father's birthday. Only Peta, the baby of the family, presented a problem.

Sighing a little as she got out of her Fiesta car at the door of the cottage, Selina hurriedly composed her face into something resembling a smile as Joan hurried forward to meet her.

'One good thing about you,' Selina quipped, 'you're even taller than me and I don't feel such a giant!'

Joan chuckled. 'I could do with your curves, young woman. I'm all angles!'

Once inside, Selina looked about for her father's rotund figure. Joan smiled. 'He's playing truant. He's been on the golf course all morning. Or so he says. I think he gossips in the clubhouse!'

'Will he be bringing his partner back to lunch?' Selina asked, as she freshened up in the pretty pink-tiled bathroom.

'We're a full house today, my dear. Not just your father's golf partner, but Peta as well.'

Selina was silent for a moment, wondering if she ought to mention Peta's antagonism towards Joan—try to explain it, help Joan to understand. Then she thought better of it. More harm than good would be done by interfering. That applied to personal relationships as well as to hospital matters. The ice hadn't thawed since the previous autumn, but that Peta was coming for a meal at all was good news.

'Couldn't you get that nice young doctor along for a meal some time?' Joan asked later, very casually, as they sat in the elegant sitting-room waiting for the others.

'Martin? Oh, he's always terribly busy. Doesn't get a moment to himself,' Selina said hurriedly.

'He can't be *that* rushed off his feet,' Joan said reprovingly. 'He's an anaesthetist. Surely they have more regular hours than your surgeons?'

Mention of 'your surgeons' brought a very different medical personage to mind. Not the stocky, red-haired and likeable Dr Martin Lenton, but the tall, dark and utterly unlikeable Elliot Richmond— and Selina was silent, her thoughts back at the Tettington with Elliot.

CHAPTER TWO

PETA ARRIVED soon afterwards, a shorter, prettier and younger version of Selina, but of similar build. Whereas Selina thought her own figure over-ample and positively matronly, she considered her little sister's shape to be curvaceous. Certainly Peta was popular with men, old as well as young, and frequently received proposals of marriage from her patients on Men's Surgical, Ward Two.

She greeted Joan politely enough, though without any real enthusiasm, but her thoughts were far away. Selina had to speak to her twice before Peta's pale blue eyes really focused.

'Sorry, Staff Nurse! Did you snarl?' she asked cheekily, and Selina aimed a playful slap at her.

'First-year students have to be snarled at!' she laughed, then glanced over at the door to the sitting-room. Her father beamed at them in the sudden silence. He was flanked by the much taller figure of Elliot Richmond.

Selina rose politely, then turned startled eyes on Peta, who jumped up and rushed forward to kiss her father, then greeted the great Elliot Richmond like an old friend!

'Elliot, dear. Dad persuaded you after all!' She linked her arm through the surgeon's, drawing him closer to the big blue velvet settee on which she'd been sitting.

Struck speechless, Selina managed only a cool smile for the surgeon, who acknowledged it with an equally cool response.

'Your father said you might be coming, Staff Nurse. I'm glad you were able to prise yourself away from the ward.'

Charles Harding raised an eyebrow at that remark, and Peta giggled and gazed up at Elliot, her eyes full of admiration. Selina coloured and swiftly turned away. Hateful man!

Peta, her own little sister, fallen prey to the charms of the worldly Mr Richmond! It was unthinkable. Again Selina wondered who Elliot had been visiting in the annexe the evening before. Peta also lived in, but in the main nurses' block, which was ruled over with a rod of iron by a home warden. No nocturnal visitors there!

Peta was nineteen, old enough to know what she was doing, and it certainly wasn't Selina's concern—but she could not help being worried. And how, she wondered, had the surgeon and the student met? Professionally, they were worlds apart. Consultants did not generally acknowledge such low life as student nurses! They must have met by chance at the house. This proved not to be the case, though, and Peta was obviously dying to tell the whole story over lunch.

Joan was an excellent cook, though she never prepared anything fancy. She believed in plain English cooking with traditional sauces, and a light pudding course to follow. It was such a change from hospital food that Selina really looked forward to meals here. She preferred to dine in comparative silence, as did Joan and Charles, but Peta could not be denied. She must always hold the centre stage, the spotlight permanently shining upon her, and the others listened with an amused indulgence as she spoke of her first meeting with Elliot.

'I burst into tears, and Elliot lent me a clean hankie!' she finished triumphantly, after giving an account of the day she nearly knocked the surgeon flying on Ward Two.

'Glad it was a clean one!' her father quipped, and Selina joined in the general laughter.

It was funny that the roast beef should taste a bit 'off' today, Selina thought. It seemed tough, too. Joan must have kept it in too long. Most unusual. She helped herself to more mustard. That was bound to help.

The boiled potatoes were just right, but Selina managed only half her serving. The heat had taken away her appetite, she found. It could not be the sight of Peta and Elliot chatting like old friends. It could not be jealousy of her vivacious sister . . . Could it? She turned the abhorrent idea over and over in her mind, just as she turned the thin slices of roast beef over and over on her plate. *Was* it possible? It was an unpalatable thought, not to be borne, and Selina quickly pushed it to the back of her mind, only to have it reappear later.

She helped Joan with the clearing away and washing-up while her father entertained the men. It did not occur to Peta to offer help, and Selina didn't want to create an atmosphere by suggesting it, so Peta was left sitting beside Elliot while Selina and Joan did the chores. Every now and again they could hear laughter from the sitting-room interspersed with remarks from Peta. Her high-pitched voice carried easily to them.

'Peta is in her element today,' Joan remarked with creditable good humour. 'Two men to captivate!'

'She must always be the leading lady,' Selina observed dryly. So dryly that Joan shot her a puzzled glance.

'Is he a special friend of hers? This Elliot chap, I mean?' Joan asked.

'I hardly know. I wasn't even aware that they'd met. Peta would have seen him on her ward, naturally, but he *is* a consultant and she's only a junior nurse.'

'Mm. Junior or not, she's made a hit there. Elliot finds her captivating, that's obvious,' Joan went on, causing Selina grievous bodily harm without realising it!

She tried hard to be pleased for her sister, but could not be. Elliot wasn't right for her. He was too old, too experienced, a man of the world. And I fancy him, anyway, she admitted. She was jealous. She could no longer deceive herself.

Not being a coward, once Selina had faced the monster, she set out to destroy it. When she and Joan rejoined the others she was particularly sweet to Peta, and smiled indulgently whenever her sister made some bright remark. To Elliot she was pleasant, but she did not monopolise him. Knowing that Peta and he would want to talk, she engaged the others in conversation. Never had an afternoon seemed so long, but as soon as she could con-

veniently and politely go, Selina left, refusing
Joan's pleas that she stay to tea. Joan and Charles
did not like a big meal at night, preferring a high tea
to dinner. Selina refused, her excuse being urgent
tasks at home. She didn't know that Elliot had
heard the exchange, and was surprised when he,
too, rose.

'Not staying to tea, Elliot?' Charles sounded put
out, and Peta was visibly annoyed.

The surgeon shook his head. 'Sorry, duty calls.
Like Staff Nurse, I also have urgent tasks.'

Selina coloured, wondering if he knew this to be
an excuse invented on the spur of the moment. She
was pleased that he wasn't staying on, but a
moment later Peta also decided to return to the
hospital.

'I'll give you a lift, Peta.' Selina brightened at the
idea of having the chatty Peta to herself for a while.
She was bound to talk about Elliot, and Selina
could listen to that sort of conversation for hours.
'If I'd known you were coming, I would have given
you a lift down here.'

'I came on the bus. I wasn't sure until the last
minute,' Peta murmured, the expression in her
eyes so pleading as she gazed at Elliot that Selina
felt that stabbing pain again. Peta did not want a lift
from her sister; she wanted Elliot Richmond to
drive her back, even though it meant going several
miles out of his way.

Elliot, to his credit, did not rise to the bait. 'I
would offer you a lift, Peta, but as your sister is
available . . .' he began, but Peta interrupted him.

'She doesn't really want to take me back,' she

said lightly. 'A budding ward sister can't be bothered with mere first-years, I'm sure!'

Selina coloured. Elliot's gaze was sharp, his eyes darkening to a stormy grey as he surveyed Selina. 'Yes. I'd forgotten you have applied for the sister's post on Ward Three,' he said reflectively, and an involuntary shiver went through Selina.

'The interviews are next Wednesday, sir,' she replied quietly, mentally cursing Peta for bringing up the subject.

'May I wish you the best of luck, Staff Nurse,' he went on, to her great surprise, and she stammered her thanks while Peta beamed at them both.

'Why don't you call him "Elliot"?' she asked ingenuously. 'Calling him "sir" makes him sound like some old greybeard!'

'Staff Nurse Harding is nothing if not correct,' Elliot smiled. 'I haven't invited her to call me by my first name, therefore she does not. However . . .'

Selina smiled vaguely, murmured a polite, 'Good evening, sir,' then turned away to take leave of her father and stepmother.

To her surprise, Peta was waiting by the car when she at last tore herself away. Elliot's big sleek Rover was just gliding down the drive and he lifted a hand in farewell as he passed them.

'If you hadn't been here, Elliot would have dropped me off,' Peta said wistfully, and Selina squeezed her hand.

'I'm sorry, pet. I didn't know you even knew the man until today.'

Peta shrugged, then her normal good humour reasserted itself. 'I haven't known him long.

Wouldn't he be a catch, though. Mrs Elliot Richmond!' She laughed, luckily not looking at Selina, who felt her feelings must be revealed in her expression.

Mrs Elliot Richmond! Whoever bore that proud man's name, she knew it would not be Peta. He would want a mature, elegant wife. A younger version of Joan, a doctor or senior nurse, perhaps. Possibly a ward sister . . .

It was a crazy notion. Anyway, she wasn't yet a ward sister. The interviews were the next hurdle.

Never had the days passed so slowly. The following Wednesday seemed an age coming. It was partly, of course, that the ward wasn't busy. Time did not actually hang on Selina's hands, but she had difficulty in keeping busy. She would be off-duty on Wednesday, though half a day would be taken up with the interview. She was due for a long weekend shortly, which would make a pleasant change.

Wednesday was Mr Richmond's round-day on Ward Three and she would miss that. He wouldn't be pleased. It was expected that sisters or acting sisters were always on duty on consultants' round-days. Guy Johns did not insist on this nicety, though usually Selina arranged to be there for his rounds. Elliot Richmond demanded the services of the senior nurse, even though in Selina's case he took very little notice of her comments.

The Senior Nursing Officer, Mrs White, came on to the ward on Tuesday, just before Elliot himself. 'All ready for the ordeal tomorrow, Selina?' She asked, as she settled herself in the visitor's chair.

Selina summoned a wan smile. 'I keep thinking about it—worrying, wondering,' she admitted.

'No good ever came of worrying,' Mrs White said briskly. 'You stand as good a chance as any of the others. The fact that you've run this ward efficiently must be in your favour—the proof of the pudding being in its eating, as the proverb goes!'

'Will you be on the board?' Selina asked hesitantly. 'I suppose you will?'

Mrs White agreed that she would. 'So will the PNO. Mr Johns was asked, naturally, but he will be away lecturing.'

'Oh! He didn't say,' Selina said in some consternation. 'I mean, he didn't tell me he had been invited.'

'Of course he was invited. He's a general surgeon and this is a general surgical ward. It was his privilege to attend, if he had been able,' the SNO pointed out, clearly surprised at Selina's agitation.

It wasn't the thought of Guy Johns that caused the ripples, it was the fear that Elliot Richmond must also have been asked! Selina moistened her dry lips. 'Mr Richmond? Has . . . I mean, will he be there?'

Mrs White nodded, and a sigh escaped Selina. 'I shouldn't have thought the consultants would . . . Is it normal practice to have them at nursing interviews?'

'It varies, my dear. At Tettington it never used to be the custom, but it seems to have grown. They aren't obliged to attend, but senior surgeons are involved. After all, they are entitled to a say in what sort of creature they're getting as ward sister.'

Selina murmured, 'Yes, of course,' and the conversation passed to more general matters.

No sooner had Mrs White left than Elliot Richmond appeared. He'd had a busy day with clinics and by now it was supper-time on the ward. And still he hadn't finished his duties.

'Any problems for me, Staff Nurse?' he asked, standing proud and aloof just outside the office door.

Colour flooded Selina's face and she wished Elliot anywhere but here. 'No . . . no, I don't think so,' she began. 'Oh! There's Mrs Austin.'

Reluctantly, she thought, he came right into the office and closed the door. 'I've got her notes here, sir.' Selina rose and handed them to him.

Because he chose to remain standing, Selina felt obliged to stand also. She wasn't that much shorter than him, she noted in some surprise. At five foot eight she sometimes felt a giant among her nurses, particularly Nurse Baxter, who could not have been more than five foot. Yet beside the tall surgeon she felt nearer average-size. Not exactly tiny and delicate, but not so big and . . .

She became aware that his silver-grey eyes were boring into hers. 'Are you ready for tomorrow, Staff Nurse?'

'I . . . Oh, yes. The interview, you mean?' Selina faltered and his lips tightened.

'Yes. The interview. I shall be there to see fair play,' he added, and Selina supposed he meant it as a joke. 'My ward round will have to begin early.'

'Mrs White said you and G . . . Mr Johns were invited, sir.'

'Ah, yes. Mr Johns,' he said sardonically. 'Such a shame he can't be there.'

Aware that Elliot was somehow getting at the older surgeon, Selina sprang to his defence before she realised the danger. 'I'm sure we will *all* miss Mr Johns and . . . and the benefit of his unbiased opinion,' she said sharply. 'He is very well thought of,' she added lamely.

'We all know how great an opinion you have of Mr Johns, Staff Nurse,' Elliot said quietly, and Selina sent him a sharp glance. 'However, tomorrow you will have to satisfy *me* about your capabilities. And I am not so easily satisfied,' he went on, grimly.

Selina went hot and cold. He was almost telling her that he would oppose her appointment! 'If I do not get the sister's post, sir, I will assume it is because there is a better-qualified or more suitable applicant,' she said, her voice shaking with emotion. 'I wouldn't want to think that personalities entered into it.'

His face darkened and Selina wished she could bite back the words. 'There *are* more suitable applicants, Staff Nurse!' he said tightly, his eyes sparking fire at her. 'However, as you are already performing the sister's tasks adequately, that must stand in your favour.'

'I'm pleased to hear you say that I'm adequate, sir,' Selina said quietly. She was near to tears, but could not let him see. Ward sisters did not break down, even when told by consultants that they were no more than adequate!

The dangerous moment passed and Mr

Richmond bent his head over the case notes again. Then the telephone rang and Selina hurriedly picked it up, almost dropping the receiver in her agitation.

It wasn't her day. As luck would have it, the caller was Dr Martin Lenton, now off duty and hoping to take her for a quiet drink in the local pub. 'Oh! No, I'm sorry,' she said shakily, 'but I can't. It . . . it isn't possible.'

There was silence at the other end. Then, 'All right. Some other time perhaps. Bye.' His receiver clicked into place and Selina was left staring at Elliot Richmond, whose silvery eyes were fixed unwinkingly on her.

It was so unusual for Martin to take no for an answer without using strong persuasion that Selina was thrown slightly. Then she realised. Because of the way she'd phrased her refusal, he had guessed there was someone in the office. Probably he would ring her back later.

Having settled that to her satisfaction, she turned her full attention to the consultant, whose gaze had dropped again to the case notes. 'Yes,' he said at last, 'there ought to be more improvement than this. When did I see her last?'

'Just before you interviewed the husband, sir. Last Friday.'

'Hm. I remember now. He's a dozy sort of fellow. Have you met him?'

Those chilly silver eyes met hers, his gaze almost challenging. An involuntary tremor wended its way down her spine. 'Only once, sir. He . . .' She hesitated, certain the surgeon didn't want her opinion, intended only to trap her in some way. 'He didn't seem very sympathetic towards his wife. Kept saying it was only a minor op and asking why she wasn't being discharged.'

Elliot's full lips tightened, his nostrils flaring with anger, and Selina felt anew the magnetism, the sheer splendour of him. Eminent surgeon he might be, but he was also a magnificent animal, a powerful, sensual man, and she caught her breath in sudden pain. He was not for her. She forced a smile to her lips as he gave vent to his anger—an anger, for once, not directed at her.

'It is not a minor op!' he thundered. 'The man's a fool! Does he think it's something I can do on a day-patient basis?'

'Probably, sir,' Selina ventured. Mr Austin struck her as that kind of man. Mrs Austin needed calm encouragement and reassurance, but received neither from her husband, a recently-retired railwayman.

'I'll have another word with him. Get him in to see me, will you?'

Selina was half tempted to tell him that it was his secretary's job, that a letter typed by her and signed by the consultant would have more force than a telephone request from a mere *nurse*. Mr Austin had great respect for authority and had several times called Selina 'Sister'. She kept correcting him and eventually it had sunk in. Selina Harding was only a staff nurse. She wasn't the ward sister and so, in his eyes, she was no more than an auxiliary. Sister's word was law, but he had no need to obey a mere staff nurse.

Not wanting to antagonise the surgeon, Selina agreed that she would telephone Mr Austin. 'Shall I do it now, sir?' She turned enquiring blue eyes upon Elliot, who smiled slightly.

'Why not? I'll wait.' To her horror, he perched on the corner of her desk while she rang the switchboard and gave the operator Mr Austin's number. He was much too close for comfort. Out of the corner of her eyes poor Selina could see those long, muscular legs clad in smart dark grey. If she leaned forward a little and fiddled with the telephone cord, she could just see the tip of one well-polished black shoe. It was agony sitting so close to him. So near, yet so very far away.

The seconds ticked by and desperately Selina sought for some topic of conversation, but nothing presented itself. Her mind was a complete blank.

Evidently the surgeon was also trying to find ways of breaking the silence, for he murmured, just as the telephone shrilled, 'Why don't you try calling me Elliot?'

Hastily Selina grabbed the phone, feeling it to be a lifeline. She was to call him Elliot! On first name terms with the great Elliot Richmond!

Mr Austin ought to have heard the pounding of her heart. It was so loud that surely he must hear it or feel some vibration coursing along the telephone wire? With as much authority as she could muster, Selina delivered her message. A day and time was fixed for the interview, the receiver replaced. She turned to the consultant with a shy smile and found his expression encouraging.

She was about to speak when there was a tap at

the office door, and Elliot hastily slid down from the desk. Selina, suppressing a giggle, called, 'Come in,' and Martin Lenton bounded in.

'Selina, dear. I couldn't understand you on the phone . . .' He stopped, his green eyes at last focusing on Elliot Richmond.

Selina blushed, though there was absolutely no reason to. It wasn't as if she and the surgeon had been interrupted behaving unprofessionally. Yet there *had* been something in the atmosphere—the beginnings of a friendship, perhaps, or at least a truce.

The anaesthetist's entrance had spoiled whatever might have been, and Elliot, after a brief word with Dr Lenton, hurried away.

Selina, tall and commanding though she was, felt like a delicate, wistful little orphan as she gazed at the closed door.

CHAPTER THREE

THE EVENING with Martin Lenton wasn't a success. Of course, there was very little evening left by the time Selina went off duty, and she did not feel inclined to sit in a smoky bar full of bright, chattering people. Martin, however, wasn't one to give in easily, and at length she agreed, mostly for the sake of peace and quiet.

The pub was one quite near the hospital. Consequently it was frequented by nurses and junior doctors. Selina's height made her immediately noticeable and, as she was a popular girl, she and Martin soon found themselves part of a much larger group.

A couple later drifted along to join them, and Selina's eyes narrowed. This evening above all she could do without the company of Staff Nurse Andrea Forman. She was with one of the administrative staff, a tall, bespectacled, sandy-haired man whom Selina knew only slightly.

Andrea greeted Selina with a delighted smile. It did not, however, reach her eyes. Selina wondered why she'd bothered to come over. Few people liked Andrea, Selina included. She hoped the younger nurse wouldn't mention the interview, now mere hours away.

That was too much to hope for. 'Soon be our big

ordeal, Selina!' Andrea began, her pale eyes watchful.

'Let's hope it isn't *too* much of an ordeal,' Selina said mildly. Then Martin reached over and squeezed her hand.

'You will be all right, Selina. Don't worry,' he said kindly. Then, as if suddenly recalling that Andrea was also short-listed, added to her, 'You, too, Andrea. You aren't going to be sacrificed to the lions! You'll be OK.'

'We can't both be all right,' Andrea said in a chilly, distant voice. 'They can't give the job to us both.'

Martin looked uncomfortable and Selina felt sorry for him. He wasn't the most tactful of men, yet he was a kind soul, good-hearted and generous to a fault. She was really very fond of him. He would make a better husband than the black-hearted Elliot Richmond. That was for sure.

She became aware that Andrea's bright gaze was still upon her. Became aware, too, that Martin's hand was still resting possessively over hers. She was surprised when Andrea didn't make some comment, but fortunately the nurse and her partner soon drifted away.

Selina was glad to go, too. She was weary, worried about the following morning's interview and, worst of all, she was afraid she and Elliot would never be as close again as they were in her office. To be on first name terms with Elliot Richmond was a privilege. That she had to call him 'sir' while her baby sister called him 'Elliot' rankled, naturally enough. If only Martin had delayed his visit to the ward. If only he hadn't come at all!

Sensing her mental withdrawal, the ebullient Martin was unusually silent on the drive back. He spoke only when he stopped his brand-new car in front of the annexe.

'Don't brood about it, Selina. Try to get a good night's sleep,' he advised, and Selina smiled wanly.

'Can *you* sleep the night before an interview?' she challenged, and he had to admit he could not.

'Try, though,' he urged. 'Going into battle tomorrow with a pale face and red-rimmed eyes won't do your cause any good!' He hesitated, then went on quickly, 'Sure I can't keep you company tonight?'

That was old ground, traversed many times before, and Selina shook her head. Whatever she felt for Martin, it wasn't love. And only in love could she spend the night with a man.

Unbidden, Elliot's cold, silvery-grey eyes bored into hers. In their depths she saw nothing; no smile, but no displeasure, either. They were as she'd seen them so often on the ward, watchful, dispassionate, probing . . .

She shivered and Martin assumed she was cold. His arm snaked around her and she made no protest when he gathered her to him. Her head dropped to his chest, and she closed her tired eyes. It was comforting. Martin was comforting. At that moment she asked for nothing more.

The interview wasn't the ordeal Selina expected. The panel already knew her work. It wasn't as if she was a stranger. Indeed, Mrs White took the trouble to say, in front of the others, that she could speak highly of Staff Nurse Harding's work and of her relationship with patients and staff.

Embarrassed but delighted, Selina had glanced away. When she was more composed her eyes met Elliot's. The chilly gaze was as she'd seen it in her imagination the evening before. No warmth lurked there, not even the faintest of smiles to ease a poor interviewee's nerves.

He could at least have smiled, she thought in sudden anger. It wouldn't have hurt him or lowered his consultant-like dignity. He must know how much the post of ward sister meant to her. Probably Peta had mentioned it to him, even if her father hadn't. She could do the job. She knew she could.

Apart from Elliot, the others were very friendly, going out of their way to put her at her ease.

Andrea had been the first to be interviewed and Selina wondered what sort of impression she had made. She knew Elliot did not care for Andrea's pert manner. Hopefully, if Selina wasn't appointed, someone from outside would be.

She would know the worst by Friday at the latest, and she kept her uneasiness to herself. There was no point in worrying now.

Thursday found Selina back on duty, on early duty this time. It was Elliot's operating day and she was rushed off her feet all morning. 'I haven't had a chance to ask you about the interview, Staff. Did you do well?' SEN Baxter asked during a lull.

Selina shrugged, wishing the older nurse hadn't mentioned it. They'd had so little spare time that, for a few hours, she had managed to forget about the interview. 'I don't know. Everyone was extremely friendly, but . . .'

Then the telephone went, and the moment passed. The unease Selina had felt at the panel's attitude remained, though. What she was about to tell Mary Baxter was that they asked a lot of questions about her private life. Was she intending to marry soon? If so, would she continue nursing? Was there any likelihood of her leaving the district? That sort of thing.

It seemed reasonable at the time. They wouldn't want to appoint a Sister who would leave for family reasons. Selina supposed they had asked all the applicants similar questions. Yet it worried her for some reason. Of course, she was able to reassure them. She had no plans to marry. Her father lived nearby so there was no reason at present for her to leave the area. If she never married, there would be no reason for her ever to leave.

Her mind protested vigorously. She *would* marry one day. Some day, some time . . .

After the patients' lunches were cleared away and the ward was quiet, Selina seized the opportunity to do some teaching. She had a responsibility to the learners, even though she wasn't the ward sister. Until her fate was known they were under her care.

As the newest patient had gall-bladder trouble she decided that should be the subject of her little talk. Jane Olphin was within a few months of taking her Finals so she ought to know about gall-bladders by now. That left Pupil Nurse Coleman and the latest addition to the ward, first-year Student Nurse

Maureen Kelly. She was straight from Introductory Block but had worked as an auxiliary in a geriatric hospital for some months, so wasn't quite green.

She seems a sensible young girl, Selina mused as they settled themselves in the otherwise deserted day-room. In build, Nurse Kelly was rather like Peta, and Selina wished she could have Peta on Ward Three. There was so much she could help her sister with. Left to herself, Selina doubted if Peta had the application, the determination to study when other more exciting alternatives were available. She was their father's favourite and how proud he would be when—*if*—she qualified.

Selina went briefly over the anatomy of the liver and gall-bladder, then on to possible causes of an inflamed gall-bladder.

Nurse Coleman was listening avidly but appeared not to understand it all, and Selina wondered if she was becoming too technical. Feeling she ought to have broken the subject down into smaller sections, she concluded the lecture.

Maureen Kelly went off happily but the pupil nurse lingered, her eyes full of questions that she wasn't sure how to phrase.

'Don't worry too much,' Selina said kindly as they strolled back up the ward. 'If at any time I become incomprehensible, just stop me. Don't let me carry on and pretend that you have followed every word.'

'No, Staff. Thank you, Staff.'

When Nurse Coleman was occupied elsewhere, Selina went quickly through the list of patients with Nurse Kelly. The student had started yesterday while Selina was at the interview and had not, as yet, been able to fix names and faces to ailments.

When Selina was off duty, a relief sister took over or a senior staff nurse, but the ward badly needed a second staff nurse. State Enrolled Nurse Baxter was capable and experienced and had often been left in charge, but it wasn't entirely fair to her. If she was a grade lower than a staff nurse she ought not to be used as one. Enrolled nurses did not have an easy time of it, as Selina well knew. The thought of Nurse Coleman ever being left in charge of Ward Three was frightening, to say the least.

'Almost half the patients are Mr Elliot Richmond's,' Selina began, and Nurse Kelly sighed, then blushed.

Another conquest for the cold-eyed Elliot Richmond, Selina reflected wryly, wondering how many more there were. 'Several of the patients are in for appendicectomy. Apart from that, we have mainly gall-bladder disease or cancer. I'll run down the list and you can make notes.'

The patient, or rather, the disorder Nurse Kelly found most interesting was Mrs Russell, who was booked for an oesophago-gastrectomy. She suffered from carcinoma of the oesophagus and her prognosis was poor. She was one of Elliot's patients and Selina thought her rather a pet. She must have realised the seriousness of her illness, yet never complained and was reluctant to bother the nurses.

'You might like to make a special study of Mrs Russell, Nurse,' Selina suggested. 'You mustn't neglect the others who have less dramatic operations, but you might not see another patient with carcinoma of the oesophagus for sometime. And I think Mrs Russell will like you.'

Indeed, Mrs Russell took immediately to the tall, fresh-faced Nurse Kelly. No matter how serious the illness, if a patient was nursed by someone who took a genuine interest, it made all the difference. Too often, patients were regarded as merely a collection of either boring or interesting symptoms. That they were also people tended to be forgotten sometimes, particularly by junior nurses, who found everything bewildering at first.

It was well after five when Selina left the ward. It was raining hard after weeks of near-drought, and she hurried across the car park, intent on reaching the annexe before she was soaked to the skin.

A voice hailed her as she ran, head down, and she turned for one wonderful moment, believing that it was Elliot Richmond's rich, deep voice. She tried to hide her disappointment when she found it was only Martin.

'Just got out of Theatre,' he panted as he came over. Rain ran down his chubby face and soaked into his sparse, reddish beard.

'Was it only a short list, then?' Selina asked, wondering how Elliot was occupying himself at that moment.

'Not too bad. Elliot's gone already. Left Ronnie to finish off an easy case. Had some pressing engagement, he said,' Martin went on, as if in answer to her unspoken query, and pain pierced Selina's heart.

A pressing engagement. With whom? she wondered.

Despite their mutual tiredness, she and Martin went out later, to the West End, to see a play Selina was keen on. That was one of the advantages of working at the Tettington. They were in the country yet within reach of the amenities of London. Martin slept through most of the play and Selina found her eyes closing half-way, but she didn't doze. She found she could enjoy the play almost as well just by listening. She could use her imagination regarding the action. One of the actors resembled Elliot Richmond, though he was not as tall as the surgeon. It hurt to look at the man and wonder where Elliot was, so that was another reason for closing her eyes.

They had supper in an elegant and intimate restaurant. Martin was an old friend of the proprietor and they were given a table in a secluded corner, away from the general chatter. It was pleasant. The wine and good food with which she was plied made Selina sleepy, and she only half heard Martin when he began to talk of a mutual colleague.

Suddenly her blue eyes snapped open as she heard the magic word 'Elliot'. 'I . . . I'm sorry, Martin. What were you saying?'

He sighed. 'I know you're tired, but you could at least listen!'

Absently she patted his hand. The gesture meant nothing, no more than if she'd reassuringly squeezed the hand of a patient. She hoped he realised that.

'I heard that Elliot didn't want you to get the Sister's post,' Martin was saying, and Selina stared at him, open-mouthed.

'Your hair looks pretty in the light,' he went on, and her hand strayed defensively to her nondescript curls.

'Nonsense. I'm only a brown mouse,' she rejoined, her mind still in a whirl. 'Do you mean that . . . that he doesn't want me to be promoted?' Her voice was faint, and she had to repeat the question.

Martin shifted uncomfortably. 'It's only a rumour, Selina, but . . . I thought perhaps you knew.'

Selina shook her head, her curls dancing. The golden lights in what she believed to be dull brown hair gleamed, turning her hair to rich golden-brown.

He sighed. 'I didn't mean to upset you, my dear.'

'Upset me?' she countered, eyes sparkling with temper. 'Why ever should I be upset? If he doesn't want me as Sister, others might.'

'Yes, that's true. I'm sure you will be all right. They can't offer the job to anyone else. It was just a rumour.'

Selina clenched her teeth. Rumours often had some foundation. The Tettington grapevine wasn't too efficient, yet . . . If Elliot Richmond had walked in at that moment she would have thrown her wine at him! Not want her to be appointed? How dare he! Surely he didn't want the vapid Andrea Forman? She was young. Pretty, too, Selina reflected. Yet it would be out of character for him to favour a nurse just because of her beauty. He wanted a mature, efficient sister on Ward Three. Ability was what counted. Evidently he didn't think she herself had enough ability. That hurt, more than Selina was prepared to admit to Martin.

When they arrived back at the annexe, it was to see Elliot's tall figure standing on the steps. A girl was beside him, laughing up into his face. The lights from the entrance hall illuminated her face clearly. It was Melanie Ovenden, a junior staff nurse who lived on the floor above Selina.

Melanie Ovenden! Selina's throat felt constricted and sudden tears welled up in her eyes. Who would have thought it?

Martin had also seen them, and he chuckled. 'Isn't that the staff nurse from Gynae? I forgot her name. She seems taken with old Elliot!'

'Melanie Ovenden,' Selina said tightly. 'I didn't realise Elliot—Mr Richmond—knew her. She's very attractive,' she added generously, but Martin merely grunted. Evidently the tall, willowy Nurse Ovenden wasn't his type.

If Martin had found Melanie attractive it would have been too much to bear. The fact that he didn't gave Selina's deflated ego a small boost. After a brief farewell kiss, she left him and strolled very slowly over to the main doors. The side-door would be locked now, so she would have to pass the couple.

Melanie had gone inside by the time Selina's reluctant feet reached the annexe. Only Elliot remained, hands in pockets as he watched her approach. He was as immaculate as ever, the dark suit tailor-made, the tie discreet. He was a highly desirable man, and Selina hated him for it at that moment.

Head held proudly, she treated him to a saintly smile and would have passed if he hadn't moved to intercept her.

'Enjoy your evening, Selina?' he asked, using her Christian name for the first time.

That threw her. Her eyes darkened with uncertainty, the pale, gold-tipped lashes half closing to shield her thoughts from his penetrating gaze. 'Yes. Yes, I did,' she murmured, wishing he would move aside so she could escape to the safety of her room.

'Come and have a coffee with me,' he commanded, taking her by surprise. Before she could think up some excuse, he had taken her arm and they were nearly at his car. Martin had gone by now and there was no one else in sight.

Unwilling to be treated like a serf, Selina refused to get into the sleek car. Elliot stared at her as they stood by the vehicle, the front passenger door invitingly open.

'For heaven's sake, get in, woman!' Gone was the superficial politeness. This was the arrogant consultant speaking, and Selina pursed her lips.

She didn't want to offend the man . . . Yet why shouldn't she offend him? She had nothing to lose. He had spoken out against her getting the Sister's post. Even if she *was* appointed it would be no thanks to him. He didn't think much of her, so nothing she said now would alter his biased opinion.

'No, I don't want to come with you, sir.' She put

all the coldness, all the hurt she felt into those few words. 'We have nothing to discuss,' she added, to reinforce her refusal.

'We can sip our coffee in silence,' he offered, his tone grim.

'No, thank you.' Her voice was firm. He must not see how much she wanted to accept. Despite the hurt he'd caused her, she still longed for him, her heart still beat dangerously fast whenever he was near.

He shrugged. Even in the faint light cast by the street lamp, Selina could see the dejected set of his shoulders, the sheer weariness. He had been operating all day, poor soul. It was spiteful of her to refuse to join him over a coffee somewhere.

Then she hardened her heart again. Hadn't he left early just to be with the delectable Melanie Ovenden? He did not deserve her compassion. 'Good night, Mr Richmond,' she said quietly, her low-heeled shoes making no sound as she hurried back towards the annexe. Her heart ached, but she would survive without Elliot Richmond.

It wasn't to be. He caught her up before she gained the sanctuary of the annexe, swinging her around to face him. Face flushed with anger, Selina opened her mouth to give him the telling-off he deserved, but something stopped her. Perhaps it was the sad, rather wistful smile he gave her. Maybe it was the warm pressure of his fingers as his hand moved from her upper arm to catch her wrist. His fingers probed gently at her pulse spot, and she could not control the tremor that shot through her.

'Let me go, Mr Richmond,' she whispered,

despising herself for not being firmer. She ought to pull away but could not.

'Call me Elliot and I might consider releasing you,' he said quietly, but she shook her head. She couldn't use his first name. It meant nothing to him, yet to her it would. It suggested a degree of intimacy, rather than the rather frosty relationship they had at present.

'I shall have to kidnap you then,' he went on, his tone even. 'Either you come quietly or I drag you into the car by your curls!'

It was starting to rain again and Selina had no more fight left in her. A cup of coffee wouldn't hurt. It would give her the chance to tell him what she thought of him, too.

Revived by the hot beverage, her temper would be more than equal to his. She permitted herself a quiet smile as she slid into the passenger seat. Let battle commence, Mr Richmond, she said silently. I'm ready for you!

CHAPTER FOUR

THE DRIVE was completed in silence. When they drew up outside a big, dark house she realised it must be his home. She should have thought. No restaurant would be open this late unless they went right into the town.

She fumbled with the catch and let herself out of the car before Elliot could assist her. When he made to take her arm she brushed him aside. She was still quietly fuming, and when the explosion came it would be the greater for having been suppressed so long.

The house was chilly and Selina wished she had a warmer coat. It was the height of summer, despite being so dreary tonight, and she wore only a thin suit of muted blues and greens, with a white knitted jacket. Without waiting for Elliot's permission, she opened the nearest door and found herself in a comfortable-looking but not over-large sitting-room. Her interested gaze took in the dark antique furniture, the big, solid table by the window, the leather-covered settee. By the table an old-fashioned standard lamp took pride of place, its pretty embroidered silk shade attracting Selina's attention. She wandered over to it, reluctant to speak to Elliot, glad to put off the moment of conflict. He had disappeared. To get coffee, she hoped. A nice milky coffee, then home to bed.

It was when she was admiring the colourful lamp-shade that she noticed the photograph. A pretty young woman laughed up at her from the photograph in a gilt frame, and Selina picked it up, wondering if Elliot had a sister, for she fancied she saw some family resemblance in the dark curly hair and large grey eyes.

There was nothing written on it to indicate that this was yet another woman in the surgeon's life, yet, without knowing why, Selina discarded the idea that this was Elliot's sister. Carefully she replaced the photo, a dull pain, almost physical in its intensity, touching her heart. She was tense, watchful, and when Elliot came up behind her and touched her on the shoulder she reacted violently, pushing his hand away as she spun round.

He looked astonished, as well he might, and Selina felt a fool. What was the matter with her? 'Got some unmentionable, highly-contagious disease, have I?' His voice was soft, but she sensed the leashed anger in him and shook her head quickly.

'I'm sorry. My nerves haven't been too good recently,' she murmured. That was no lie.

He turned away. 'Perhaps you ought to see a psychiatrist. A surgeon won't be of much use to you.' He disappeared, and an angry Selina hurried after him, finding him in a long, narrow kitchen-breakfast room. It was decorated in dark colours, though the furniture here was modern enough. She perched on one of the high stools by the breakfast bar and watched him make the coffee.

Neither of them spoke until the coffee was ready. Politely he asked whether she preferred to drink it there or in the sitting-room, and she chose to remain where she was. The stool was comfortable and she felt less at a disadvantage here.

He sat at the other end of the Formica-topped breakfast bar and busily stirred his coffee, his dark head bent. He had put out a plate of fancy biscuits but Selina had eaten too well to be tempted by anything more than coffee.

'You will hear tomorrow, I should think,' he said abruptly, breaking the fragile peace. Selina's left hand balled into a fist and she was glad he couldn't see it.

'Yes, I expect so,' she said quietly, meeting his gaze.

Those handsome silver-grey eyes swept over her dispassionately. 'I hope it will be good news.'

That was too much. Such hypocrisy! 'Do you?' she challenged. 'You didn't want me to get the post! It's no secret. You can't deny it!' She waited, eyes flashing, hoping against hope that he *would* deny it.

A faint smile moved across his sensuous mouth, then was gone.

'Well?' she demanded, incensed because he made no move to defend himself.

'Well what?' he enquired mildly. He reached for a custard cream and bit into it.

'I was told that you don't want me to be Sister on Ward Three,' she went on, controlling her temper with an effort.

'If that's what you heard, it must be true.' He finished the biscuit and began to stir his coffee again. He seemed in complete control, yet she sensed that he was rattled and was trying to hide it. The coffee didn't need quite so much stirring.

'But why? Why? Am I such a poor staff nurse?' she cried, wanting to understand his reasons even while she deplored them.

'You are adequate. I've said so before.' His tone was bored, as though he'd had enough of the conversation—enough of Staff Nurse Harding as well.

Tears welled up but she would *not* cry in front of the man. It was an old feminine trick, and he would despise her for it. She would despise herself, come to that. Briefly she thought of Peta. *She* wasn't afraid to use all the feminine tricks in the book. And the arrogant Elliot Richmond had lent Peta a hankie. Fat chance there was of him lending one to her big sister!

He gauged her thoughts accurately. 'Why don't you shed a few tears, Staff Nurse? It runs in the family.'

'It isn't likely you would lend *me* one of your hankies,' she said lightly, her anger evaporating in sorrow. If she cried, she would be left to weep alone.

'Peta has the advantage of youth and beauty, plus a charming personality,' he said bluntly, and Selina closed her eyes in pain. 'I'm sure Martin Lenton would be delighted to mop up your tears,' he went on remorselessly, and her eyes snapped open.

'No doubt he would,' she agreed sweetly, and saw him redden. She slid off the stool, having drank less than half the coffee. 'Thank you for your hospitality, sir. It was . . . adequate,' she added slyly.

His face darkened. She'd hurt him, but derived no satisfaction from her victory. He didn't like her. He thought her incapable of becoming a good ward sister. And he considered her personality anything but charming. That hurt more than anything.

His dark, brooding presence followed her to the sitting-room. She could have reached out and touched him. How she wanted to touch him! Merely the pressure of his fingers would have been enough, the touch of his hand, an intimate smile. She had no right. Whoever he belonged to, it wasn't Staff Nurse Selina Harding.

Her eyes went straight to the framed photograph. She longed to ask him if the girl was a relation, but did not dare. He would quite likely tell her to mind her own business. She picked up her jacket, wondering if she dared mention it. Would asking about the photo show him how desperate she was to know? Would this arrogant man read more into her interest than there was?

Playing for time, Selina put her jacket on, wondering if he would take her home. It was on the tip of her tongue to refuse. She could telephone for a taxi. She *would* telephone for a taxi!

'Pretty girl,' she murmured as she carefully did up the buttons on her jacket, then glanced about for her bag.

'You noticed then?' His tone was as casual as her own and she smiled brightly at a point somewhere between his body and the doorway, carefully avoiding his eyes.

'I was admiring the lampshade. Then I saw the photo,' she said lightly, unable to delay her departure any longer.

That's . . . Jane. My fiancée.'

The dull heart pain was back and Selina felt faint. It was her own fault. Hadn't she almost asked him to spell it out for her? She had no one to blame but herself.

To her utter disgust he didn't offer her a lift. Instead he picked up the telephone with a muttered, 'I'll order a taxi for you.'

Her blue eyes grew bigger and rounder. She couldn't believe it. To bring her out to his house for coffee, then to abandon her. It was unbelievable!

That she had intended refusing a lift from him, she ignored at that moment. If it was *her* choice to return by taxi that was different, but to be given no choice at all!

Elliot put the receiver down, his face a frozen mask. 'He's coming directly.'

'I could have phoned Martin. He would have been delighted to pick me up,' she said quietly. Indeed, she wondered why she hadn't thought of it before. Then she dismissed the idea. She couldn't haul poor Martin out of bed. He wouldn't be pleased to know she had rounded off her evening in Elliot's house, anyway.

'Shall I cancel the taxi, then? Do you wish to ring Martin?'

'No!' she snapped. 'It was just an idea. I can't get the poor soul out of bed just to give me a lift home.'

'I doubt that he would mind. I expect you do

favours for him,' he put in. 'You are very good
friends.'

'Yes. We are,' she said firmly. In reality they
were no more than acquaintances. Let Elliot think
there was more to it than that. Let him believe that
she was almost engaged. It would be something else
for the Tettington grapevine to stew over.

Rather than remain in the sitting-room, Selina
preferred to stand in the front doorway despite the
cold breeze. She wanted no favours from Mr Elliot
Richmond.

The headlights of the approaching taxi caught
her, then swept by as it came to a halt. So soon. She
was sorry to see it, sad to leave this hateful yet
somehow appealing man.

'I would have offered you a lift back,' he said
softly, and her startled gaze seemed to amuse him,
for he smiled. 'In the circumstances, I thought
better of it.' He hesitated, but the moment was
gone. The taxi was waiting.

'Good night, Staff Nurse,' he said formally, as
she got into the taxi. 'Pleasant dreams.'

Pleasant dreams indeed! He must know she
would not sleep a wink all night, wondering what
the morning's post would bring.

As she stood by her lonely divan later, Selina
wished fervently that Elliot had kissed her.
She believed he meant to. She wondered
what the touch of his lips would be like. He had
a beautiful mouth, the lower lip full and sensual,
the upper firm and harsh. A determined mouth
belonging to a determined man. She began to
tremble, whether from the chilling evening or

from reaction, she didn't know.

It was wicked of her, expecting him to kiss her. He was, by his own admission, engaged to be married. If *she* was his fiancée she would hit the roof if she found him in another woman's arms!

Once she was undressed and in her plain white cotton nightie, she went to stand miserably in front of the long mirror in her tiny bathroom. She turned this way and that, subjecting her body to intense scrutiny. Was she *so* repulsive? True, she was big. Tall and generously-curved. Yet she kept her body in trim with regular exercises. Her face and hair were ordinary, she had to admit. A small, straight nose, an average sort of mouth, blue eyes. Nothing special there. Her hair was naturally curly but that could be a trial sometimes. If she had long, straight hair she could do so much more with it. Put it up in an elegant chignon, perhaps. Or a french pleat. Elliot might admire her then.

Sadly she turned away, padding barefoot back to her tiny, cramped bedroom. Wishing would get her nowhere. Whichever way she looked at it, she was very, very average, and in no way likely to attract the tall, dark and dynamically handsome Elliot Richmond.

She was a fool. He would marry his pretty grey-eyed Jane.

Morning came at last. Selina had slept fitfully and wakened almost as tired as she went to bed. She was on early duty, too, and didn't really feel up to it. But duty called, and somehow she made it on time. Luckily the uniforms were easy to get into and she hadn't to struggle with a starched collar and ridiculously small collar-studs as in the past. The new uniform did nothing for her figure, but she mustn't grumble.

They were busy, which was probably as well. An emergency admission came in before the ward-work was organised for the morning. Unfortunately, Nurse Baxter was on days off and Selina had to make do with an inexperienced staff nurse. Staff Nurse Michaels was willing enough. Pleasant, too. Selina wondered how the girl had ever passed her State Finals, though, for 'efficiency' was a word unknown to her.

It was Mr Johns' round-day, which didn't help. Guy Johns had never been known to appear early for a round. He always began punctually at nine-thirty. Indeed, Selina had heard it said that patients on Ward Three could set their watches by him. On this fateful morning he arrived nearly twenty minutes early and nothing was ready.

If SEN Baxter had been there, Selina would have been ready for him by nine, but as it was she was at the other end of the ward with Staff Nurse Michaels, the younger nurse having called her to look at Mrs Asher, a lady in her fifties with inoperable carcinoma. She was due for discharge home as nothing could be done for her. Radiotherapy had been discussed with her husband, but the idea abandoned. Mrs Asher was Guy Johns' patient and to him there seemed no point in causing the woman inconvenience and further suffering. Measures would be only palliative, and radiotherapy meant a long journey to the Regional Centre, Tettington not having the facilities. Mrs Asher would return home to die as peacefully and painlessly as possible, cared for by her husband.

Nurse Michaels had called Selina because Mrs Asher was crying, something she did frequently, even though she didn't know she was dying. The woman's eyesight wasn't too good and as she did not recognise the new nurse she had begun to cry. Nurse Michaels' soothing words served only to increase her grief and uncertainty.

When a harassed Selina emerged from behind the bed-curtains it was to see Guy Johns strolling down the ward, chatting to patients as he went. The colour left her face and she began to apologise. Friendly and sympathetic he might be, but he *was* a consultant and she ought to have been ready for his round.

'I'm dreadfully sorry, sir,' she began, but he smilingly brushed away her apology.

'Not to worry, my dear. I am a little early.' He followed her into the office, humming a dance tune under his breath, one that Selina recognised. It was a favourite of Peta's.

'Can't get that dratted tune out of my head,' Guy complained, easing himself into Selina's chair. 'One of my boys keeps playing it.'

'So does Peta. She's brought her record-player from home and I hear that tune every time I pop in to see her.'

'How is she? I hear Elliot is taking an interest in her.' Guy began to read the Kardex, unmindful of the bombshell he had just dropped.

I hear Elliot is taking an interest in her. Now

where did he hear that? Surely lending the girl a hankie to stifle her sobs didn't mean he was physically attracted to her? It was ridiculous. Quite ridiculous. Yet that remark stayed with Selina throughout the ward round.

She was preoccupied after the round. Once the consultant and entourage had departed, she sat at her desk, the round-book open in front of her. Guy didn't mention Peta or Elliot again, and she hadn't liked to broach the subject. Was Elliot interested in Peta? But she was so young! Then Selina remembered Melanie Ovenden. She couldn't be more than twenty-one or twenty-two. Elliot liked them young, or so it would seem. But what about Jane? And, more important, who *was* Jane? *Where* was Jane?

Just before lunch, Mrs Lofts died. She had been very poorly before her operation and not much better after it. She had been in ITU and had returned to the ward only the night before. She was Guy's patient and Selina was glad of that. He would cope in his amiable way. Elliot would have suffered with the bereaved husband. Would have gone through agonies of doubt, as well, wondering if he ought not to have operated. Yet without the operation the woman would have died from the carcinoma. There was little choice, though the operation had offered some hope. Guy would look at it that way. He—and the patient—had taken the only chance there was. Mrs Lofts had known of the seriousness of her condition and had shown rare courage. Selina saluted her memory.

It wasn't that Guy didn't care. He did. His was a

warm, caring personality. He was more extrovert than Elliot, though, and never needlessly bottled up his feelings. Some you won and some you lost.

A sombre Selina went back to the ward after lunch, a hurried and unsatisfactory meal. She was, she discovered, rather like Elliot. She took things too much to heart. She was sad over the death of Mrs Lofts. So much so that the afternoon was well advanced before she realised—the eagerly-awaited letter hadn't come! She swallowed her disappointment bravely, and although she was quieter than normal, none of the patients commented upon it, so she must have *looked* the same.

The letter was delayed because it was a letter regretting that she had not, on this occasion, been successful, Selina decided. That was the reason. The successful applicant would receive a letter first, and once she had accepted the post the others would be notified.

Andrea Forman worked on Ward Two at present. Selina's hand hovered over the internal telephone, wondering if she dared ring. Yet what could she say? If Andrea had heard, she would have lost no time in telling everyone. Selina and Ward Three would have been her first point of call, there was no doubt of that.

During the period when the late-duty nurses were at tea, Andrea called into Ward Three, her long, narrow face petulant. Selina greeted her calmly, trying to hide her pleasure that Andrea hadn't heard, either. She could bear anything but that.

'Have you heard, Selina?' Andrea's voice was

casual and Selina quickly put her out of her misery. 'I haven't heard either,' Andrea went on, her lower lip drooping.

'I suppose you will be coming here as staff nurse, if not as sister?' Selina said, not relishing the thought. Andrea brightened.

'Yes, that's true. There are loads of changes I want to make.'

Selina flushed. 'It's still my ward, Andrea. When the new sister comes I expect I shall stay on as staff nurse. Until another post becomes vacant, that is,' she went on determinedly. If Elliot didn't want her to stay then she would not. Without the consultant's whole-hearted co-operation she could not work.

Then the telephone shrilled, and Andrea hurried away, still looking annoyed at Selina's reminder. Andrea would not be the senior staff nurse on Ward Three and that would never do. Selina doubted that the girl would stay on the ward.

The telephone call was a summons from the PNO, Mrs Taylor. It was the PNO's secretary, so Selina couldn't ask why she was being summoned. She was told she need not go until she finished her duty, so it could not be anything very important.

A summons from the Principal Nursing Officer was always worrying, though, and Selina silently went through a list of possible misdemeanours. Elliot Richmond. Had he complained to Mrs Taylor? Yet of what could he complain? He might not like her, but as far as she knew she hadn't misbehaved, had done nothing in particular to bring down his wrath upon her.

She met Peta as she was flying down the endless corridor towards the administrative offices. 'Hello, Selina! You look all hot and bothered. Have you heard yet?' Peta, all shining-eyed and happy, clutched at Selina's arm.

Selina shook her head. 'Not yet. I expect they will tell the successful applicant first. Then the rest of us will hear.' She managed a brave smile. 'How is your studying going?'

'That's what I wanted to say. One or two of the girls are coming to my room later for a study-bee and I told them you would come along and help,' Peta announced, her eyes fixed pleadingly upon Selina.

Selina hesitated. On top of her disappointment, there was an interview with the PNO. Now this. She was to spend her precious evening with a load of giggling students. A refusal hovered on her lips, then she bit it back. After all, wasn't that what nursing was all about? You studied, you learned, you gained experience, then you taught others. As a senior staff nurse it was part of her job to teach learners.

Teaching the new generation was a privilege as well as a duty. One day, if ever she became a ward sister, she would expect to do even more. Clinical instructors were always thin on the ground and teaching was, after all, the traditional prerogative of sisters.

She made arrangements to see Peta later, then hurried to the PNO's office, glad that Peta was studying that evening. For if she was at her books, she could not be out with Elliot Richmond.

CHAPTER FIVE

SELINA walked back from the interview in a daze. She, Selina Harding, was to be Ward Three's new sister! That was the reason for the summons. Mrs Taylor wanted to give her the letter personally. The Principal Nursing Officer's congratulations still rang in her ears as she strolled back to the annexe. Sister Harding!

Once back in her flatlet she read the letter again, still unable to believe it. Out of all the well-qualified, experienced applicants, they had chosen her! The only cloud upon her horizon at that moment was Elliot Richmond. Mrs Taylor had made it clear that Selina was *her* choice, but felt obliged to point out that the decision was not unanimous. Somehow a rumour had got around that Selina and Dr Martin Lenton were on the point of becoming engaged. Naturally the committee wished to appoint someone who was either married or fancy-free, Mrs Taylor had explained.

'Naturally,' Selina had murmured in reply, trying to hide her anger. She recalled the way Andrea Forman's eyes had lit up at the sight of Martin patting her hand. Yet the rumour must have started before that. Could Elliot Richmond be the culprit?

Mrs Taylor didn't say which members were against Selina's appointment. She didn't need to. It was so obvious. Elliot Richmond thought her only just good enough. He also believed that she and Martin were good friends, possibly even lovers. He wouldn't want the post to go to a nurse who was simply fooling around. Sister on Ward Three must be a person who would throw herself whole-heartedly into the job, whose mind wasn't half on her social life or her loved one.

She sighed as she reread the letter, some of her happiness evaporating. Now she had two enemies—Elliot Richmond and Andrea Forman. Never had she felt so alone. Never did she feel less like a studying session with her young sister.

She tilted her head a little higher. She would show them, prove to Elliot that she was far more than just 'adequate'. No matter what problems the next few days brought, she would manage some-how. She hadn't come all this way only to falter at the first real obstacle. She vowed that she would make Elliot Richmond glad that she had been appointed.

The weekend was quiet because they had several vacancies. Selina suspected that they would be full again by the middle of the week. In the meantime it was good to have a breathing space. She took the opportunity to chat to all the patients. After visi-tors, on Saturday afternoon, she and one of the students played Scrabble with two of the patients. Selina wasn't good at word-making and the student, Jane Olphin, won easily, with Selina trail-ing behind the patients. She did better at Snakes and Ladders, but unfortunately had to leave the game when she was nearly home, with only two more snakes to escape.

She rattled the dice, intent on throwing a five, which would have seen her first home. So intent was she that one of the patients, Mrs Bradley, had to nudge her. Elliot Richmond was an interested spectator of the game and Selina hadn't realised he was there.

Once made aware of the fact, she rose quickly, her face flushed. One more black mark against Selina Harding. She neglected her nursing and administrative duties to entertain the patients. That would never do!

Unrepentant, Selina gazed back at him innocently. In her eyes there was a challenge. She was daring the great man to comment or to criticise her. Something showed in his silver-grey gaze. A flicker, no more. Selina almost believed it was approval, but that she would never receive from Elliot Richmond.

Excusing herself from the game, she escorted him to her office, wondering at this unexpected visit from a consultant. And on a Saturday, too. She hadn't realised he was even in the hospital. So near, yet so far. A prickle of awareness made its way up her spine, then down again. She could smell his aftershave. Onyx. Her father used the same one, and Selina liked it.

Elliot was casually dressed in cords and dark green shirt and jacket and was without a tie. She'd heard the subdued sighs, the murmurs from the ladies as they passed through the ward to the office. She knew the feeling only too well. Even in his casuals he was sexy, oozing a kind of arrogant, ruthless charm. No wonder the female patients sighed!

Once the consultant was comfortably seated, Selina turned to him with a distant smile. 'What can I do for you, sir?' she asked coolly. She wasn't going to fawn over him and he needn't think she was. If this was the day for home truths, so be it.

He settled back in the visitor's chair, arms behind head, eyes half-closed. He had remarkably long lashes. They were thick and black, and glossy like satin. A beautiful frame for his beautiful eyes, Selina mused. Then he glanced up and caught her staring.

Embarrassed, she took refuge in frowning and trying to look severe. With her round face and open countenance this was difficult, and the surgeon actually smiled. The smile spread across his lean, handsome face and then he grinned, his sharp white teeth glinting.

Selina went crimson. She could do nothing to stop the flush that spread over her face and down to her ears and neck. Her whole body felt hot, and she lashed out at him in self-defence.

'I'm glad you find me amusing, sir,' she said bitingly. 'What would you like me to do for my next trick? I could stand on my head or turn cartwheels,' she went on, recklessly. 'Or would you prefer me to crack a few jokes? For an encore, I could . . .'

'For God's sake, Selina!' Elliot jumped up and Selina took a step backwards, thinking he was about to strike her. Indeed, he seemed half-inclined to do so. His fists were clenched by his sides and his eyes blazed down into hers.

'Why can't we be friends?' he asked brokenly,

but Selina had no answer. Friends was what they could never be. They could be enemies or lovers, but never friends. There was too much electricity passing between them for anything so mundane as friendship.

'I should hate to think we were enemies, sir,' she said, keeping her voice even. It was an effort, but he would never know.

'So should I, Staff Nurse,' he agreed, his tone as neutral as her own. 'Though I suppose I should call you Sister now. May I offer my congratulations upon your appointment?'

The silvery eyes were cold now, and Selina knew he didn't want to congratulate her. They were just so many empty words. 'Thank you, sir,' she replied politely enough. She hoped he would forgive her earlier outburst, though she certainly wasn't about to apologise. The wretched man had driven her to it!

Elliot wandered about the room, her troubled gaze following him. He was restless, on edge, and she wondered why. Then someone knocked gently on the half-open door, and he swung round. It was Melanie Ovenden, and Selina almost choked.

'Are you ready, Elliot?' the girl asked shyly, her adoring gaze fixed upon the consultant.

He nodded. 'Whenever you say, pet,' he answered, his voice a caressing murmur.

Selina managed to smile at the newcomer, though she was sure the smile was frosty and forbidding. Her jaw muscles ached with the effort and her face felt stiff. With a distant smile for Selina, the surgeon left, and she could hear Melanie's light, carefree voice until the couple passed through the swing doors.

Elliot and Melanie. Or Elliot and Peta? The man was a rake! And what about poor Jane? Jealous though she was of the unknown Jane, she began to feel sorry for her. She was half inclined to warn Peta, but thought better of it. It smacked of sour grapes. And at nineteen one did not take kindly to advice from one's elders, no matter how well-meaning.

Later, Selina had another unexpected visitor. Little Pam Hargreaves, the blind girl who had been a patient there recently. She was now completely recovered.

Selina was delighted to see her, for the girl had been her favourite patient. Pam was accompanied by her doting mother and elder brother. Selina hadn't seen the brother before as he was away on a course during Pam's stay in hospital.

Derek Hargreaves was nice, Selina decided. He was about her own age, tall and on the thin side, with molten brown eyes Selina would have liked herself. He teased his sister good-naturedly and obviously idolised her. Selina's eyes grew sad for the girl, who had been blind from birth.

Although Pam and her mother had left a big box of chocolates for the nurses when Pam was discharged, Derek wanted to give them a little token now. His face was flushed and Selina felt sorry for him. She hoped the mother hadn't persuaded him to give money. That simply would not do. She had her refusal ready, kind but firm, but he surprised her. It was a party he was offering. He wanted to invite all the nurses on Ward Three and their boyfriends, plus any of the surgeons who might care to drop in.

'My little sister keeps telling me that nurses get lousy food!' he chuckled. 'Chips with everything, a surfeit of beefburgers and so on. I thought we could make up to them in some way. Lay on some *real* food!'

Selina was delighted with the idea. Those nurses who lived in would welcome a change of diet. As hospital canteens went, Tettington was about average. With so little money available and staff cut-backs, she thought the catering department did as well as could be expected. One did not expect prime grilled steak on a hospital menu.

A date was fixed for the party and Selina promised to ask all the staff, plus any who might have left the ward since Pam was discharged.

'Will the surgeon with the lovely deep voice come?' Pam asked wistfully, and Selina didn't need to ask *which* surgeon.

'I'll see that Mr Richmond is told of your invitation, Pam,' she promised. 'Does the invitation include the anaesthetist, Dr Lenton?'

'Oh yes, of course. The operation wouldn't have been very comfortable without an anaesthetic!' Pam laughed. 'And the theatre staff, too,' she added.

Selina thought that was rather too many for an intimate party, but apparently they had lots of room in the house. If the weather was fine the guests could spill out into the garden. Derek Hargreaves told her one of the neighbours had a swimming-pool which Pam used regularly, swimming being one of her few pleasures. He reckoned the neighbour, if invited to the party, would offer the staff the use of his pool for the evening.

It all sounded rather grand. Selina wondered where the money was coming from for the party, and offered to make some sausage-rolls or whatever they might fancy, but Derek wouldn't hear of it.

'You just bring yourself,' he said warmly. Rather too warmly, Selina thought. When they parted, he shook hands, letting his hand stay in hers longer than was necessary. She found herself blushing like a schoolgirl. Even Peta didn't blush any more, and that fact made Selina feel like a big, over-grown child.

The week passed slowly. Andrea Forman returned from her off-duty to find that Selina had been given the post, after all, and she sullenly presented herself on Ward Three on Monday afternoon. She was to be working there from the following Monday and was keen to see what days off she was to have.

Andrea wasn't very forthcoming, but she did offer her congratulations on Selina's appointment, so it might not be as bad as the new Sister had feared.

Wednesday was a bad day. It was Elliot's round, of course, but it didn't start there. Selina's terrible day actually began the previous evening. Joan had telephoned to invite her to a 'good square meal', as she put it.

Selina was on early duty and would finish by five,

and accepted the invitation with pleasure. It was stretching the truth to suggest that nurses thought of nothing except food, but she enjoyed Joan's cooking. She was also tired of her own company. A quiet evening with her father and stepmother, a milky drink and a biscuit before driving back to the hospital—what could be more peaceful? The idyllic scene she'd pictured did not include her sister and the consultant, but they were there when she arrived, and she tried hard not to mind.

'Elliot's helping Peta with her homework!' their father chuckled. 'Do you think he's serious?' he went on. Selina tried to give a carefree laugh, but it didn't quite come off.

Charles peered at her. 'Not sickening, are you? I've heard there's a new strain of flu on the way.'

She shook her head. A healthy young person would survive a dose of flu. She wasn't sure she would survive if Elliot became her brother-in-law!

She felt she ought to mention his fiancée, but that would be underhand. She might let Peta know casually, when they were alone. Yet if Elliot was keeping the engagement a big secret, telling the chatty Peta might bring down his wrath upon them both.

Elliot was, naturally, staying for the evening meal. It was for his benefit that dinner was being provided instead of high tea. He and Peta emerged from the study in time for pre-dinner drinks. He greeted Selina coolly but without surprise, his eyes hooded, and she gave him a tight smile in return.

She had to admit he was looking very desirable. He was wearing one of the formal dark suits he favoured, though this one had a matching waist-coat. It fitted him well, the cut of the waistcoat emphasising his broad chest and flat abdomen, the well-cut trousers moulding his long, athletic legs. She couldn't blame Peta for being mesmerised. Or Melanie Ovenden, come to that.

Reluctantly Selina dragged her eyes away from the surgeon, and asked her sister about the study-ing session. Peta put her glass down and beamed.

'Abdominal surgery! That's the thing. We've loads of interesting cases on Ward Two at the moment, though most of the older men are in for herniotomy.' She leaned forward. 'Do you know, there's a Mr White who—'

'Leave names out of it, Peta.' The surgeon spoke commandingly, and Peta laughed.

'Sorry. It's unethical, I know. Must not gossip about patients in public places!'

'This is hardly a public place,' Selina put in, immediately going to Peta's defence, 'but outside you must never mention patients' names or discuss their innards. The person sitting next to you in the café or behind you in the bus or train might be a relative of the person whose clinical details you find so amusing! That's what we were taught in PTS.'

'What a sensible tutor you had, Sister Harding,' Elliot put in dryly, and Peta giggled.

Selina fought down her anger. The surgeon's words made her feel about an inch high. Peta didn't seem to mind him occasionally being sharp with her, though. That became noticeable as the even-ing wore on.

The meal was superb, as always. Joan served

them enormous steaks, with mountains of fresh vegetables. For those who wanted them, including her father, there were duchesse potatoes, but Selina refused, mindful of her figure. Put up against the svelte Andrea Forman she knew she appeared large and clumsy and must diet severely.

Selina felt sad watching Elliot and Peta. Try as she might, she could not keep her eyes from straying towards them during the course of the evening. They argued happily together, rather like an indulgent uncle with his favourite niece. Not that Elliot would feel avuncular towards the pretty Peta, of course.

Once or twice he spoke sharply to her, but she took it with good grace, shamelessly flirting with the man. Then she mentioned Hal Sayers, one of the students in her group. Selina knew Hal slightly. He was a pleasant, if rather feckless, boy. She doubted if he came up to Peta in intelligence and would not be a steadying influence on her.

Yet the girl was only nineteen! Did she *need* a steadying influence? Selina decided she did not. She also decided that Elliot was far too worldly-wise for her sister, but she could do nothing, say nothing. She mistrusted her own motives.

'I'm off next weekend, Selina,' Peta's high-pitched voice broke into Selina's thoughts, and she tried to appear interested.

'Are you doing anything special?' She, too, would be off for the weekend, a long weekend for her. And oh, how she needed that break! She was sure she had aged considerably while waiting for the result of the interview.

'Mm. Hal and I are off to Bath. They're having a special weekend. Some literary do, I think. Georgian England.'

Selina was surprised. 'I never knew you were keen on literature.'

Peta laughed. 'It's Hal's mother. She wanted to go and she roped him in. He wouldn't go without me. He's devoted to me,' she went on, with a sly glance at Elliot. 'In a puppyish sort of way, of course.'

'Of course,' Selina agreed, wondering if Elliot would take the hint. Hal was too young, too immature, she implied. She preferred older men. The message was unmistakable, but Elliot didn't seem to hear. He was deep in conversation with Charles on a golfing topic.

Selina left soon afterwards. She offered her sister a lift back to the hospital but it was abruptly refused. 'Elliot's taking me out for a drink. Then I daresay he will drop me off at the Tettington. The longest way round, naturally!'

Selina wanted to shake her and very nearly did. Only the timely arrival of Joan saved Peta from a severe talking-to. She had no right to lead Elliot on in that way! It was selfish of her.

She said goodbye to her father and Joan and was about to get into her small car when she saw Elliot approaching. His stride was firm, purposeful, and she supposed he had something to say concerning the following day's round.

They traded glances, Selina struggling to keep hers neutral.

'I shall be rather late tomorrow morning, Sister

Harding,' he said at last. They were back to 'Sister Harding' again. Poor 'Selina' must be out of favour.

He turned away and a voice called him back. Selina did not at first recognise the voice as her own. It was more like a cry of anguish, and she blushed once she realised.

He moved nearer, one heavy brow raised. 'You wanted me, Sister?'

How true that was! Selina could hardly get the words out. She did not know where to begin. 'It's Peta, sir,' she blurted out at last.

His eyes became colder, and she shivered. She could feel the ice from where she was standing. He made no comment, did not try to make it easier for her, and she lost her temper. She couldn't raise her voice in case the rest of the family heard, so she hissed instead. 'You've no right to pretend an interest in her! She's young and . . . and . . .'

'Rather immature. Was that the description you were seeking?' he asked politely, and she bit back the words she wanted to utter. Don't antagonise the man! Remember, Selina, he didn't *want* you on Ward Three, and if he tries hard enough he can have you removed.

Having to appear humble was painful and alien to Selina's outgoing nature. 'Yes. She *is* immature, sir, and . . . and very young.'

He folded his arms and gave a long drawn-out sigh. 'We have established that your sister is young and immature. What else can we say about her character? Let's see, now.' He leant on Selina's car, too close for comfort. 'She likes being the centre of attention,' he carried on, almost to himself. 'She doesn't care whose feelings she hurts . . .'

'That's it!' Selina found her voice again. 'She didn't *mean* to hurt you. She just wasn't thinking. That's no crime!'

'Forgive me if I appear puzzled . . .' Here he leaned closer, and Selina tried to move back a few steps, but his arm prevented her. He had her trapped very neatly between the car and the wall which divided the house from its neighbour. 'I wondered if we were still discussing Peta's short-comings? You now seem to be defending her.'

'Yes, well,' she mumbled. Elliot's nearness was upsetting her train of thought. The rational thoughts in her head were rational no longer.

'Selina, look at me,' he commanded.

Obediently Selina met his gaze. His expression was unfathomable. 'I have no interest whatsoever in Peta. As you have pointed out several times, she *is* immature. She simply is not my type.'

Relief rushed over her and she smiled, the smile lighting up her rather plain face, transforming her, did she but know it. She did not become beautiful, but her lovely blue eyes sparkled and her generous mouth curved invitingly.

Even a strong man like Elliot Richmond wasn't immune to such charm, and he bent his head swiftly and kissed her. His lips touched hers briefly, tanta-lisingly, and the pain in her heart was unbearable. So brief, so quickly over. She choked back a sob, then his questing mouth found hers again. In the distance she heard Peta's voice, and abruptly they broke apart.

Damn Peta! Selina thought angrily. He might have kissed me again if she hadn't spoiled it. She had difficulty in opening her eyes. In truth, she didn't want to open them, to face reality again. Being in Elliot's arms was wonderful, no matter how brief the embrace. Now he had released her she was cold, bereft. Back to 'Mr Richmond' and 'Sister Harding' again, she supposed.

They were still standing close together when Peta approached. Her eyes narrowed as she stared at them. She may have suspected something, but Selina doubted it. It would not occur to her that her big sister might attract the darkly handsome Elliot Richmond.

'You shouldn't discuss weighty surgical matters when you're off duty!' Peta joked.

'What makes you think we're discussing surgery?' Elliot asked mildly. 'Selina and I *do* have other topics of conversation.'

Peta flushed, and Selina wanted to hit the man. Even if he didn't fancy Peta he had no right to torment her. She obviously cared for him. 'Come on, Elliot,' Peta coaxed, 'don't keep Selina. She has to get back to the hospital.'

With a wry smile for Selina, Elliot allowed himself to be led back to the house, and her eyes followed him, much as her heart wanted to do. Whether Elliot realised it or not, Peta had him set up to be her fiancé at the very least. If he had no more sense than that, he deserved his fate! That was Selina's final thought before she got into her car and made her way back to the annexe and to her lonely flatlet.

Without Elliot, everywhere was lonely. She would survive, continue to exist somehow, she supposed. For if Elliot wasn't interested in Peta it did not mean he *was* interested in her big sister. There was still Jane.

Wednesday dawned fine and clear. It was a lovely morning as Selina walked over to the hospital. One of those 'good to be alive' days. It was Elliot's round, and that alone lent a spring to her step as she swept through the swing doors, eager to start.

The night nurse eyed her gloomily, and just for a second Selina's eagerness dimmed. Then she inwardly shrugged. Whatever it was, she would cope somehow.

'They've hardly slept a wink all night,' Nurse Frost intoned. 'I don't know why. Though once one patient becomes unsettled it has a chain effect.'

Selina nodded. 'It spoils the day for them, too. They become edgy and irritable. And every time they try to settle down for a nap, some nurse comes along with a squeaky trolley!'

Apart from that, there were no problems, so the round ought to be a quick one.

Elliot was only a few minutes late, and Selina greeted him with a smile, to be met by an ominously curt nod. Keeping her smile pinned to her face wasn't easy, but she wasn't going to let him see how he'd upset her. Behind the consultant's back, his senior registrar shot her a warning glance.

It was going to be one of those days, evidently. Before the round they went through the list of Elliot's patients. That wasn't right, either. Whatever minute fault he could find, he pounced on.

'Mrs Gibson, Sister Harding,' he said tightly, and Selina tensed. She was due for discharge following a sub-total thyroidectomy. A very difficult, demanding lady still. She ought to have been discharged the previous day, but had refused to go. Elliot must have known that.

'Yes, sir?'

'She is to be discharged, surely? I thought she'd gone. Why hasn't she gone?' he demanded, rounding on Selina, who sat by the side of her desk, Elliot having appropriated her place behind it.

'Because she . . .' Selina began.

'I want no excuses, Sister!' he thundered. At least, it sounded like thunder. His disapproval always did, even though he never raised his voice. 'Have we so many vacancies that we can afford to keep people when they should be at home? Doesn't she *want* to go home?'

'No sir, she does not,' Selina said calmly, though she felt anything but calm.

Silence fell, and Elliot looked discomfited. 'I'll see her,' he said heavily, then closed his notebook with a snap. 'Come on, I haven't all day!'

Selina and the registrar exchanged wry glances. The morning wasn't going to get any better, it was going to get worse.

CHAPTER SIX

THINGS DID get worse. The patients did not suffer because of Elliot's mood, of course. Yet they sensed an atmosphere and responded accordingly, saying, 'Yes, sir,' 'Of course, Doctor,' 'Oh no, naturally I wouldn't, Doctor,' and so on, in sub-dued tones. One or two of them gave Selina a sympathetic smile as she passed, and she felt com-forted. She prayed that everything would go like clockwork and that Elliot's bad humour would fade. He wouldn't praise her, no matter how well-oiled the ward machinery, how smooth the round. All she could hope for was a lack of criticism.

That criticism came eventually. They were at Mrs Gibson's bed now and Selina almost crossed her fingers. Mrs Gibson, though difficult, was an attractive woman and Selina rather liked her. Only the junior staff didn't get on with her. She was a woman of superior intelligence and a lively per-sonality and she delighted in playing off one junior nurse against another. It was fun to her, Selina supposed, but the youngsters didn't see it that way.

After asking Mrs Gibson how she was, Elliot settled himself in a hastily procured chair by the bed. 'I informed your GP that you were to be discharged.' He bent his head over his notes and wrote.

Mrs Gibson nibbled her lower lip. 'Yes, but I'm really not quite right. I need another few days, Doctor,' she insisted, plucking at his jacket sleeve.

Selina closed her eyes momentarily. Whatever annoyance Mrs Gibson caused him, you could take bets that it would be Selina who would suffer.

He glanced up, frowning. 'According to your notes you should have gone home yesterday but wouldn't go. Is that right?'

Mrs Gibson nodded complacently, then winced. 'My neck still hurts, you see. And the scar hasn't faded yet. And my voice!'

'The slight hoarseness is only temporary, Mrs Gibson,' Elliot reassured her. 'I'm sure Sister has already told you that.'

'No, I don't think so. I can't seem to recall . . .' she began, and Selina wanted to scream. Of course she had explained to the woman, had tried to reassure her—but it was no use defending herself. Elliot would believe the patient.

He conducted a gentle examination, just to reassure her that everything was being done. Then, somehow, he managed to persuade her to agree to discharge.

'We'll leave it for today. Try to get a good night's sleep. Then you will be fit and eager to be off home tomorrow.' With a kind smile for her, he stepped outside the curtain and proceeded down the ward, leaving Selina to catch up as best she could. He really was a trial this morning!

Back in the office he rounded on Selina, who stood her ground. The light of battle was in her eye and she could be formidable when she chose.

Surgeon and Sister glared at each other, while the rest of the staff tried to become invisible.

'Why wasn't I informed that Mrs Gibson refused to go home?' Elliot launched straight into the attack but Selina knew she was in the right.

'I telephoned your secretary, sir,' she replied firmly. 'Surely you received the message?'

He shook his head. Then the registrar, Ronnie, put in quietly, 'Sister told me as well, sir. I was about to mention it but . . .'

To her chagrin, Elliot did not vent his ire on the registrar. Oh, no. He must lay the blame at Selina's door. He was in the process of telling her what he thought of the lack of communication when there was a confident rap on the door and Andrea Forman appeared.

She seemed taken aback at the sight of the consultant, and Selina gave her the benefit of the doubt. She may not have known it was his round-day. Once she realised, she ought to have left immediately since her business wasn't important. But she stayed, treating Elliot to a rare smile.

'I'm so sorry, Mr Richmond,' she cooed, 'but Sister changed my off-duty and I wanted to make sure that . . .'

Elliot exploded. 'This is hardly the time to fix the duty-roster! Come back later—when Sister has had time to sort herself out.'

Selina's blood boiled. She was in the wrong again! Andrea retired with a hurt expression, and Elliot, tight-lipped, wrote up the rest of the notes, then disappeared with a curt, 'Good morning.'

Why, he hadn't even drunk his coffee! Selina

gazed in dismay at the door he had so firmly closed behind him. Yesterday, a kiss; today, a beating. Hurt and bewildered, yet trying not to show it, she raised an eyebrow at Staff Nurse Michaels.

'That's that. Goodbye and thank you, Mr Richmond!' she said lightly, and the nurse giggled.

'What a man! Mr Johns isn't a bit like that. He's all soft and cuddly. I . . . I mean, he *looks* soft and cuddly,' she amended hastily, and Selina tried not to smile. She was right, Guy Johns had a friendly teddy bear look. Yet Selina wouldn't swop Elliot Richmond for all the friendly teddy bears in the world!

Later, she began to wonder what Andrea Forman had meant about changing her off-duty. On Monday she was to start on Ward Three. Nursing officers arranged the duty rota, not ward sisters as in some hospitals, so if a nurse wasn't satisfied with the off-duty she was given she had to fight it out with the superior. If the new nursing officer had altered Andrea's off-duty it was hardly Selina's fault, but she needed to know.

After contacting the office and finding that the rota hadn't been changed, Selina almost phoned Andrea and asked her to call in. But why should she? The damage was done now. Elliot believed she was so incompetent that she muddled up nurses' days off. Yesterday seemed far away, and the memory of his kiss, his touch, was fast fading.

Elliot put in another appearance on the ward while most of the nurses were at tea. Those on early shift finished at five and were not entitled to a tea-break—an official one, that is. If the ward was quiet and she had enough staff, Selina liked to let them all have a short break, and she did so today.

When Elliot arrived there were only herself and Nurse Olphin on duty, with two of the others due back at any moment. Naturally that was wrong in his eyes. Selina had to concede that he was in the right this time, but if she was at all worried about the patients she wouldn't have let the morning shift nurses have a break.

'It is, after all, *my* ward,' she put in gently, after he had told her she was incompetent. He hadn't dressed the word up. That was the one he'd used. Incompetent.

'If I doubted that Student Nurse Olphin and I could manage I would not have sent the others off the ward, Mr Richmond,' Selina went on, sticking out her determined chin. 'Had we been very busy, I doubt that anyone would have had a tea-break,' she added for good measure. 'A few minutes snatched on easy days makes up to the nurses for the majority of days when they're rushed off their feet.'

'All right, all right,' he groaned, giving a broken smile. 'I surrender, Sister Harding!'

Her deep blue eyes opened wide. What a change! She just could not fathom this man.

He stood by the big window in the office, having refused a chair. From her seat, Selina had an excellent view of the ward and could be there instantly if required. At the moment Nurse Olphin was sitting by Miss Wise's bed, chatting to her. Several of the others were gathered around. The visiting hour was over and those patients who could get up were either in the day-room or strolling about the ward.

Selina supposed it was an untidy scene. The old-type sisters wouldn't have liked to see patients wandering about the ward. It was a cosy picture, though; the ladies were as happy as their conditions allowed them to be, and that was what mattered.

She noticed Elliot's gaze on the student, and was ready with words of defence if he told her that her staff shouldn't be so informal. He was right. He nearly always was, and that rankled.

'A nice contented ward you have, Sister,' he said instead, and Selina's mouth opened but no words came. Praise indeed! She nearly said so, but bit back the hasty words. This is paradise, Selina, don't spoil it, she admonished herself.

'How is Mrs Bolton doing? I found her depressed this morning,' Elliot said quietly, turning back to face her. His expression was friendly for once, and Selina gave him her opinion.

'She needs to be up and doing. She's an active little soul, sir. She . . .'

'Couldn't you call me Elliot now? After all, you *have* risen a grade.'

'No thanks to you!' she snapped before she could bite her tongue. She watched, horrified, as dark colour swept up his face.

'Oh, no! Elliot, I didn't mean it. I . . .'

'At least you managed not to call me "sir". *That* makes a change!' he replied. He opened the door and she jumped up, prepared to drag him back into the room if necessary. They mustn't part this way!

'I apologise,' she said stiffly. 'Do you want to see

Mrs Bolton again?' She was willing him to close the door and he did so, a faint smile crossing his face.

'Ah, yes. Mrs Bolton. That was the reason I returned, wasn't it?' He perched on the arm of her chair so Selina had no option but to stand by the window. She could sit on one of the chairs kept for visitors, but felt ill at ease. Every time she saw Elliot, the picture of Jane seemed to float beside him. Who *was* she?

She frowned and glanced out at the ward again. All seemed well. Mrs Gibson was holding court with three other patients. Her sore throat must be better. Then her eye alighted on Nurse Olphin, her pretty, dark-haired student. She was called Jane!

No, it couldn't be! His Jane had a small, heart-shaped face, whereas Nurse Olphin . . .

'Could you spare me a few seconds of your attention, Sister?' Elliot's sarcastic voice brought her back to earth. After a few moments' discussion of Mrs Bolton's partial gastrectomy, Elliot rose to leave and Selina could think of no excuse to keep him this time.

There was a visitor outside the door, and she was about to smile a welcome when she realised who he was. Derek Hargreaves, Pam's brother. It was then that she remembered the party invitation. She had undertaken to invite Elliot and it had slipped her mind. Little wonder with all the fights she and the surgeon were having. Parties were the last thing on her mind!

'Oh, Mr Richmond. This . . . this is Mr Hargreaves. He's the brother of Pam Hargreaves, the young blind girl you operated on.'

The two men shook hands, and Selina eyed them covertly. Elliot was by far the taller of the two and he looked years older, as well. Derek Hargreaves had an open, frank countenance and rather soft features. Elliot's face was lean and hard, ruthless even, with its strong straight nose and forceful chin. Yet he wasn't that old. She put him in his mid-thirties, no more.

'Sister has told you about the party, I expect?' Derek said politely. 'Are you able to come, sir?'

Selina coloured, aware that Elliot must be totting up the number of her misdemeanours.

'Oh, yes. The party. A lovely thought,' Elliot said affably, and Selina let out her pent-up breath. After thanking Derek Hargreaves for the invitation, Elliot left without another glance at Selina. Quickly she blinked back the tears which threatened to spill over at any moment. How embarrassing if she cried in front of her visitor.

Derek moved nearer, his steps unsure. 'Are you all right, Sister?' His brown eyes were concerned, and Selina was touched by his kindness.

She smiled wanly and offered him a seat. 'I'm fine, really. But I'm desperately tired. It's been a terribly busy day,' she added, hoping he would take the hint and not stay.

He got up immediately and apologised for coming at all. 'I know you nurses never get a minute to yourselves. Especially ward sisters,' he added, with an admiring glance at Selina's new cap, the lace pill-box worn exclusively by sisters. She hadn't yet been given the navy blue tippet or shoulder cape, but eventually the sewing room would get around to it. She still had the same white dresses which were worn by all nursing ranks. Around her waist the navy blue petersham belt denoted her registered nurse status, as did the ornate silver buckle, which her father had bought her when she qualified. Selina wore it with pride.

Derek hesitated, and Selina wished he would go. 'I was thinking . . . About tonight. I mean—would you like to come for a drink?' he finally blurted out, and she was able to refuse without regret. She wanted to return to her little flat and have a good cry.

'I've had a dreadful day, Mr Hargreaves,' she replied, knowing it to be the truth. 'All I want this evening is a hot bath and an early night. I'm worn out.'

'Of course you are. I expect you are run off your feet,' he said soothingly. 'But I wanted your help with young Pam.' His face clouded over for a moment. 'I promise not to keep you out late. You can rest in the pub,' he assured her.

Selina went white with anger. She was tired. She'd had one hell of a day, and on top of that she had quarrelled with the man she secretly loved. She didn't want to spend her precious free evening in a noisy smoky pub!

When she began to protest, he merely beamed at her and arranged to meet her outside the hospital later that evening. Even then, Selina could still have refused. If it had been anyone else forcing an invitation upon her, she would have said no most emphatically. Yet she had a soft spot for Pam, and the brother seemed concerned. Yes, she would go.

It might do her good. Better than staying at home and brooding about the hatefully handsome Elliot Richmond.

Derek Hargreaves took her to the pub near the hospital. Selina would have preferred a venue further away. She didn't want to bump into hospital people, but of course she did so. Andrea Forman was there with her boyfriend, and she smiled maliciously at Selina. At least, Selina decided the smile was malicious. She may have been doing the other girl an injustice. Because she was tired and overwrought, everything, every slight, every glance or smile, became magnified and grew into something else.

When Derek took her hand gently, Selina snatched it away. Her nerve-ends were frayed and she chose to believe that he was getting fresh. In a calmer mood, she would simply have made a joke before moving her hand. Tonight she could not do so. He flushed and stared down at his drink, a lager.

Selina similarly stared fixedly at hers, which was a Martini. She sipped it very slowly, intending to make it last all evening, and hoped 'all evening' would prove to be no more than another half-hour or so.

'You wanted to talk about Pam,' she prompted, when the silence went on.

'Yes. Pam. She's proving rather difficult, Sister.' He laughed shortly. 'I can't take a girl out and call her Sister Harding! What's your first name?'

'Selina, Mr Hargreaves,' she said quietly, wishing someone would let off a firework. Anything to get the man moving.

'Selina,' he repeated. 'That's a beautiful name.'

'Yes, isn't it? Now, what about Pam?'

'She's taken up with—oh, good evening, Mr Richmond!' He rose hastily, and Selina turned startled eyes towards the newcomer.

Elliot gazed down reprovingly, and Selina felt like a small child caught scribbling on the best wallpaper. Beside him stood Melanie Ovenden. 'I'm glad to see you are enjoying yourself, Sister Harding,' he said pleasantly. His silver eyes were cold and belied the tone of his voice. Selina wasn't fooled.

'I'm having a wonderful evening, thank you, Elliot,' she retorted, deliberately using his Christian name. Sink *that* putt, her eyes challenged.

A smile tugged at his mouth as he replied, 'Don't let your fiancé know what an enjoyable evening you're having, will you?'

With that, he and Melanie passed by, Selina's startled gaze following them.

'I didn't realise you were engaged, Selina.' Her escort's tone was reproachful.

'It's hardly relevant, is it? We are here to talk about your sister and her party, Mr Hargreaves,' she said sweetly. 'My personal life isn't under discussion, surely?'

A ruffled Derek Hargreaves agreed that it wasn't. All the time he was talking about his sister, Selina's mind buzzed with the one word—fiancé. *What* fiancé? If she was engaged, no one had told her. Surely Elliot didn't mean Martin? There was nothing between them. She felt nothing for him save warm friendship. Far different from what she felt for the enigmatic Mr Richmond!

'The Martians are landing tonight.' Derek Hargreaves' voice finally penetrated her involved and muddled thoughts and she stared at him in astonishment. 'They're landing in my back garden,' he said grimly. 'I told you so about five minutes ago, and you nodded and smiled.'

Selina flushed guiltily. 'I'm sorry, but my chief's remark threw me for a moment. I . . .' She was about to say that she didn't know she was engaged, then thought better of it. 'I didn't realise he knew about the . . . the engagement,' she said instead.

Then she had to listen to him repeat his tale. Pam fancied herself in love, and her brother didn't know what to do about it. Nor did their mother, and she had suggested they should consult Sister Harding.

'The boy she loves—is he not suitable? Is there an age difference?' Selina asked, and Derek frowned.

'He's in his twenties. Pam met him through the club she belongs to. He's a voluntary helper there.'

'That sounds promising. What is it you have against him?'

Derek denied that they had anything against him, and Selina frowned. 'I thought you said he wasn't suitable?' Had he? Perhaps *she* had suggested that. 'There must be something wrong with him if you aren't happy about the romance,' she added. Surreptitiously she glanced at the clock. Another ten minutes or so and she could politely make her escape.

'It isn't him, it's *her*! Pam. She's blind! She needs taking care of for the rest of her life. She can't possibly marry. She couldn't cope. Quite out of the question,' Derek went on grimly, and Selina could hardly believe her ears. 'That's where you come in, Selina.'

'I do? What do you expect me—'

He cut in. 'We want you to persuade him to drop her. It's no use talking to Pam. She's a stubborn little thing.'

Good for her, Selina mused. She was on Pam's side, but nothing would be achieved by saying so. She must play it by ear. She agreed to talk to the man but pointed out that they could not live Pam's life for her.

'You surely wouldn't expect her to cope on her own?' he asked. His voice had risen and Selina shot him a warning look.

'It's time we went, I think. I've had an extremely tiresome day,' she said meaningly.

'I suppose I *have* been tiresome,' he said ruefully, rising. 'But we're so worried. You're our only hope, Sister . . . I mean, Selina.'

She smiled. 'Will he be at the party?'

He nodded emphatically. 'Pam insisted. She said he would love to meet all the doctors and nurses. His name's Howard, by the way.'

It was probably just a passing attraction. He was kind to Pam and she was grateful and had mistaken kindness and gratitude for love. Selina thought of Peta, the same age as Pam. She must get the two of them together. It would do Pam good. At nineteen she was rather young to be considering settling down, or so Selina decided from the vantage point of those extra seven years.

They left the bar without seeing any more of Elliot and his friend, but he must have been watching, for he was only a few steps behind them when they reached Derek's car, a Capri.

'Sister Harding, may I speak to you for a moment?' Although the request was framed as a question, no question was implied. Elliot wanted to speak to her and she must obey.

Inwardly rebelling, Selina swung round, fearing to see Melanie hanging on Elliot's arm. But he was alone. Relieved, she waited. So did Derek Hargreaves, though he gave an impatient sigh.

Elliot had keen hearing and his eyes turned accusingly upon Derek. 'As you are in a hurry, Mr Hargreaves, I'll take Sister home, shall I? Save keeping you,' he went on, giving Derek the benefit of his charming smile.

Derek began to protest, but Elliot didn't let him finish. Selina merely stood there, an impassive observer. Naturally she preferred Elliot's company, but the prospect of sharing the car with Staff Nurse Ovenden did not appeal. However, she was given no choice. Elliot was accustomed to winning.

She found herself saying good night and thank you to Derek. Then her arm was gripped just below the elbow, and she was marched towards Elliot's blue Rover.

CHAPTER SEVEN

'LET ME GO!' Selina hissed. 'You're hurting my arm!'

'I *am* sorry,' Elliot retorted sarcastically, and she began to struggle, her temper overriding common sense.

He took no notice of her futile attempts to escape, and when she heard voices behind them as a group of people left the pub, Selina ceased to struggle. It would be embarrassing if someone tried to rescue her!

When they reached the car, she found to her relief that Melanie was nowhere in sight. 'What about Nurse Ovenden?' she demanded truculently. 'You haven't left her in the bar, surely?'

'She's sitting with some friends.'

Selina subsided into the front seat. It was rude of him to leave his date just to give his ward sister a lift home, Stupid, too, for Melanie lived in the same building.

'I wanted to talk to you,' he began as he started up the car. His voice was strained, and Selina glanced at him in surprise.

'What about? Was it Pam Hargreaves' party? Or my so-called engagement, perhaps,' she added dryly.

'I apologise for jumping the gun, Selina. I know it isn't official yet so . . .'

Selina fumed quietly, noticing that ahead of them was Derek's Capri. She had seen him pull out of the car park just before them. He was heading in the same direction and driving fast.

'Damn fool!' Elliot's voice broke into her painful musings, then her horrified gaze saw the Capri swerve off the road. She heard a woman scream, then blackness descended before she could identify the woman's voice as her own . . .

She was recalled to the world by Elliot's voice. She was half dreaming. She must be, for she could have sworn she heard him call her 'my darling'.

'Selina!' No mistaking his voice now. With an effort she opened her eyes and met his flint-hard gaze.

There was no tenderness there and she felt like weeping. So much for dreams.

'What happened? Oh! Derek—is he hurt?' But Elliot was already out of the car, cautioning her to stay where she was. He didn't, she thought resentfully, even stop to ask if she'd broken anything. Luckily she hadn't. She must have blacked out for a few seconds.

Outside it was turning dusk and all was noise and chaos. Shaking her head to clear it, Selina got groggily out of the car which had stopped only millimetres from Derek's vehicle. It could have been so much worse. His car had slewed across the road and ended up facing the opposite way. By some miracle, no other vehicle was involved, but there were two other cars there now, their drivers offering assistance.

Derek was shocked and dazed and had grazed his left arm, but appeared otherwise unhurt and was able to walk unaided to Elliot's car. Selina settled him in the the back seat and sat beside him on the remainder of the journey to the hospital.

She remained by his side while he was attended to in A and E. She felt he ought to be admitted for the night, but no one else thought so, and he was told to report back if he suffered any headache or unnatural drowsiness.

'Mr Richmond, couldn't we offer him a bed?' Selina asked hesitantly, when Derek was pronounced fit to go.

'He can come home with me,' he said shortly. 'I suppose you let him drink too much!' He rounded on her so savagely that she couldn't think straight.

'He hadn't been drinking!' she managed at last, but Elliot, tight-lipped, was already turning away. He took Derek home with him, after phoning the garage to pick up the car. Presumably Elliot would return to the pub for Melanie. Selina hoped he hadn't forgotten and did not feel inclined to remind him.

Once back in her flatlet, she sank on to the edge of the narrow bed. Her head and limbs ached. She felt she'd been stretched on a rack and had just been released. With a sigh she lay back against the pillow and closed her eyes.

She drifted between sleep and wakefulness. She could hear Elliot's voice calling, 'My darling,' over and over again, and she smiled as she drifted off to sleep once more, wondering what he had been trying to tell her.

Selina overslept. She was due on early shift but hadn't set her alarm. After years of early rising she woke early automatically, even when she was on late shift, but the accident and her tussles with Elliot had worn her out and she slept on. It was gone eight when she roused herself the following morning and half-past by the time she arrived on Ward Three, after a hasty wash and no breakfast, not even a cup of coffee.

She'd telephoned the ward and explained that she'd overslept. Elliot Richmond answered the phone. It was his operating day and he had called on the ward to check up on a patient. His tone was cold and measured but not noticeably angry. Indeed, he asked how she was. After assuring him she was fine, she began to ask after Derek Hargreaves, but Elliot put the phone down with a clatter, and a tired and agitated Selina was left holding the receiver.

Elliot had gone to Theatre by the time Selina arrived on the ward. 'He seemed concerned about you, Sister,' SEN Baxter told her, her shrewd blue eyes on Selina's ashen face. 'Said you weren't to overwork today and he hoped to see you tonight as arranged.'

'We haven't arranged anything! I . . . I hardly know the man!' Her face was ashen no longer, it flamed, and Nurse Baxter smiled kindly at her.

'If the great white chief says something has been arranged, that's that!' SEN Baxter bustled out of the office, leaving a shaking Selina to pull herself together.

Staff Nurse Michaels, prompted by SEN Baxter,

had the ward running properly and Selina was grateful. There were three patients from the ward to go down to Theatre and Mrs Gibson was to be discharged at last. Selina hurried down the ward to her bed. It was empty but not yet re-made, and she tracked her down to the bathroom.

Mrs Gibson was alone in the bathroom but perfectly capable of managing. Nevertheless, Selina wasn't taking any chances. She delegated Pupil Nurse Coleman to offer her any assistance she required.

'See that she has everything she needs. Don't let her linger in the bath,' Selina said quietly. 'Is she packed?'

'Oh yes, Sister! She started before breakfast. She's all ready.'

That was something. Selina nibbled her lower lip thoughtfully. She ought to get the bed remade, just in case . . . Then someone waved to her from the main ward door. It was Derek Hargreaves, and she found it hard to hide her annoyance.

She strode up the ward towards him, trying to smile a welcome but not making a very good job of it. 'How are you? No headache?' she queried, and Derek shook his head gingerly.

'Not too bad, thanks. Good job your chief was behind me. He must have quick reflexes.'

'I'm sure he has,' Selina said dryly. 'He thought you were drunk last night. I hope you convinced him otherwise?'

His smile was rueful. ' "One lager, sir," I said! Even offered to walk the chalk line!'

'Did he say he was going to Pam's party? We . . .

we haven't had a chance to discuss it.' If Elliot was going, who was accompanying him? That was what she wanted to know.

'Yes, he seems keen.' That was all Derek said on that subject, and Selina didn't like to press him, to ask if Elliot was bringing a partner.

She intended seeking out Pupil Nurse Coleman, who was, she assumed, still in the vicinity of the bathroom, but then the telephone rang and by the time she had dealt with the query, Mrs Gibson was back in her bed, settling herself comfortably. She did not intend to be discharged today, either!

Wearing a tolerant smile, Selina walked calmly down the ward. The other patients were whispering among themselves, but Selina ignored their comments. She ignored Mrs Gibson as well. The woman craved attention. Well, she wasn't getting any!

In the sluice she found Nurse Coleman, with tears pouring down her thin cheeks. One of the auxiliaries was with her.

'There! Here's Sister now,' she said as Selina entered. 'She'll know what to do.'

Because she was Sister, naturally she would know what to do. Ward Sisters knew everything!

'It's Mrs Gibson, Sister. She won't go! She . . . she says she's a tax-payer and if she needs a h-hospital bed then she's entitled to one. She says she's stopping till M-Monday!' poor Nurse Coleman sobbed. The auxiliary enfolded her in her motherly arms, and a bemused Selina wandered into the bathroom to give herself time to think.

Well, Sister Harding, and how are you going to cope with *tha*?

She knew what she ought to do. Tell Mrs White straightaway. That was defeatism, though, and Selina did not intend to be defeated. Somehow or other she must cope by herself—but how?

After some more thought, Selina retraced her steps, passing close to Mrs Gibson's bed but not looking at the woman. Once back in her office, she flicked through the case notes. There was a phone number for Mr Gibson. She had spoken to him on Tuesday. Twice, in fact. Once to tell him his wife would be getting a taxi home, the second time to tell him his wife wasn't coming!

He sounded resigned once Selina had explained the situation to him, and arranged to come during his lunch-break.

Just before lunch she got Student Nurse Kelly to pick up Mrs Gibson's belongings. The case wasn't in evidence but Nurse Coleman had told her she'd seen the patient packing one and she certainly hadn't been seen to unpack it.

Selina watched discreetly as the tall Nurse Kelly approached Mrs Gibson. She saw them exchange a few words and heard the student laugh. The case was retrieved from behind the locker, and Nurse Kelly brought it to the office.

'Mrs Gibson says she isn't going today, Sister. But I laughed and said that's a rare joke. We've casualties coming in this afternoon. Everyone's going who can walk,' Nurse Kelly announced calmly, setting the case down.

'Don't say that, even in a joke!' Selina pleaded.

'Thank you for your efforts. I'll see to her now.'
The nurse had done as she was asked. Selina
thought sending a junior would be the best solu-
tion. If she saw Selina herself approaching, Mrs
Gibson would dig herself in more thoroughly, and a
scene was to be avoided at all costs. While it would
entertain the fitter patients, it could harm the
weaker ones. Selina had a responsibility to *all* her
patients.

Mr Gibson duly arrived, grinning from ear to
ear, and a happier Selina was able to reassure him
that his wife was ready to go. By this time, Nurse
Kelly had winkled Mrs Gibson out of bed and had
remade it as an admission bed. Luckily, two other
patients were to be discharged that day, both being
Mr Johns' patients, so the woman could see that the
ward *was* emptying as she'd been told.

Yet it was unethical of the student to lie to her
about casualties needing the beds, and it worried
Selina. Later on she would take the girl aside and
caution her against repeating her error. At the
same time, she was relieved to be getting rid of a
trying and difficult patient. Elliot would have
blamed her if she'd let the woman stay even a few
hours more, yet she had the dreadful feeling that,
even now, she hadn't heard the last of the affair.
Mrs Gibson was trouble with a capital 'T'.

All through the day Selina was conscious of Elliot's
message—that he would see her tonight as
arranged. But they had arranged nothing! He'd
given her a lift home because he wanted to talk to
her, but Derek's accident had spoiled that. Perhaps

Elliot intended coming to the flat to finish the conversation.

Selina was perplexed. She could not imagine what there was to discuss. Anyway, she wouldn't invite him to her flatlet. They would have to talk in the communal lounge, a big room used by all the trained staff. The television was usually on as well, and there was no privacy. It would have to do. The last thing she wanted was a private conversation with the surgeon. Or worse still, an evening out. She must make that quite clear.

Because she was afraid of being alone when—*if*— he came, Selina stayed in the lounge longer than she'd intended. The TV was on, though she took no interest in the programme. There were three others in the room and they kept up a desultory conversation. Then the others drifted away one by one and Selina was alone. Hastily she switched off the set, then gathered up her *Nursing Times* which she had intended to read. Elliot mustn't catch her unawares.

She almost bumped into a man as she hurriedly left the room and stepped back a pace, excuses trembling on her lips.

Martin Lenton eyed her in some surprise, and she coloured. 'Oh, it's you! I . . . I thought . . . Did you want something?' Selina amended hastily. He mustn't know she was expecting a very different caller!

'Hardly killing the fatted calf for me, but I'll excuse you,' Martin said mildly, shrewd green eyes on her flushed face. 'Were you expecting someone else?'

'No! No, oh no. No, I wasn't, but . . .'

'One "No" would have been sufficient, Selina,' he said, and she gave him a brilliant smile to cover her confusion. It saved talking as well. The least said, the better.

'I thought an intimate little dinner *à deux* somewhere. Does that appeal?'

Did it appeal? She wasn't sure. At least it would give her an excuse not to go out with Elliot Richmond.

'I . . . I thought I would have an early night, Martin,' she found herself saying instead. 'I overslept this morning and I'm not really dressed for wining and dining.'

She looked down at her comfortable old skirt and blouse, and his gaze followed hers. She had kicked her slippers off and her legs were bare. 'You have remarkably sexy toes!' Martin chuckled.

'Martin! Only chiropodists notice toes!' Selina laughed in spite of herself. Martin was good for her and took her out of herself. She *would* go out with him and damn Elliot Richmond! Before she could tell him of her change of mind, Elliot himself appeared. He hovered in the doorway, Selina and Martin having moved further into the room.

Martin put a friendly arm around her before she had quite registered the other man's presence. She was trapped!

Elliot and Martin eyed each other, and Selina went cold. They were friends, or at least acquaintances. There was no emnity between them, so she wasn't afraid they would fight to the death over her, but even so it was a delicate situation.

'Yes, they *are* sexy,' Elliot observed quietly, and she nearly choked. 'Particularly the great toe on the right foot.' He bent over a little, the better to observe Selina's feet, and she tried to hide her right foot by standing on one leg like a flamingo. His cold, silvery eyes met hers. 'I hope you aren't coming out barefoot, Selina?'

'Coming out? Is she?' Martin rumbled, and Selina felt trapped again. 'I've just invited her out and she said she was having an early night.'

Selina blushed furiously, the more so when Elliot remarked with a hint of steel in his voice, 'Selina isn't having an early night with me, if that's worrying you. I wanted to talk to her. There are one or two matters we have to discuss and there never seems time on the ward,' he went on casually.

'You surely don't expect her to talk shop on her evening off?' Martin was scandalised.

Selina stood mutely, waiting for them to come to a decision. Obviously she wanted to go out with Elliot, but, realising the dangers, she would be better off with Martin. On the other hand she might wash her hair and have an early night after all. It would serve them both right if she did!

'I'll leave you to chat then,' she said suddenly. 'Good night, both.' She flew into her room before the men could comment. Carefully she locked the door behind her and leaned against it, her heart pounding.

She so wanted to hear what Elliot had to say, particularly if it concerned the mysterious Jane. Yet she could hardly go out with him now. Having refused one, she must refuse both. She almost stamped her foot in frustrated rage, but thought better of it.

Elliot, Elliot! If only you knew how much time I spend day-dreaming about you! The fact that if he did know he wouldn't care, made it all the more heart-breaking.

Disconsolately she padded into her tiny bath-room, towel in hand. She would wash all her troubles away. Rather like Nellie in *South Pacific*, she was going to wash that man right out of her hair!

Selina was just wrapping a towel about her wet hair when there was a knock at the door of the flatlet. She tensed, wondering which of them it was. When a female voice called out, 'Telephone, Selina!' she let out her pent-up breath. They must have gone. No doubt Martin was ringing to demand an explanation. She had none to give him—that was the trouble.

She unwrapped the towel and unlocked the door. Still barefoot, she ventured into the hall—to find Elliot Richmond leaning nonchalantly against the banisters. 'I thought you were getting ready, Selina,' he said reproachfully, a glint of amusement in the silver-grey eyes.

'I . . . I shampooed my hair,' she muttered, taken aback.

'Yes, I can see that. Hurry up, there's a good girl.'

'Hurry up for what?' she demanded, swiftly recovering. 'I'm not going anywhere with you!'

'You aren't going anywhere with Martin, that's for sure,' he countered smoothly. 'He's given up and gone home.'

'Gone home?' she echoed, wondering what threats Elliot had used on him.

'Yes, he lost.'

'Lost?' she repeated foolishly.

'We tossed a coin and I won. I'll wait while you dress.' Elliot made a sudden movement and Selina shrank back, afraid he was going to wait in her flatlet.

His lips tightened ominously. 'I'm not trying to coerce you. I'll wait here. How long will you need?'

Relieved, she blurted out, 'About twenty minutes. Oh, I have to dry my hair! I forgot,' she went on mournfully.

He sighed. 'I sometimes think you were *born* awkward. Just to plague consultant surgeons,' he added slyly, and her temper rose.

'I'm sorry Martin lost,' she said bitingly, before retreating into the room.

Hastily she plugged in her small hair-dryer. Luckily her hair was naturally curly or Elliot would have had to wait for hours. She couldn't stop to dry it completely, but it would have to do. She didn't know where he was taking her, probably just for a drive around, so there was no need to wear anything special. Even so, she naturally wanted to look her best for him. She longed for an outfit to make her appear small and dainty, and the nearest she had was the silky printed suit she was wearing when she first heard of Jane. She doubted if Elliot would remember that he'd seen it so recently, and it did marvels for her figure and morale.

At about the appointed time she inched open the door, half-wondering if Elliot would still be there.

He was. So was Melanie Ovenden. They sat on the stairs, and Melanie was patting his hand. Selina was so angry she almost shut the door again, but Elliot was already rising, a disturbing smile on his face. She controlled her annoyance with some difficulty, but bestowed a charming smile upon Melanie. If it did not reach her eyes, no one noticed.

'You took long enough,' Elliot muttered as he escorted her out of the building. He did not comment on the suit, nor did he tell her how pretty she looked. Not that she considered herself pretty, of course, but a little white lie wouldn't have hurt him!

They were in the car before she remembered the telephone call. 'What about my phone call? Who was it? Did they hang up?'

'Phone call? Oh, that.' He smiled disarmingly white teeth gleaming. 'I got one of the nurses to tell you there was a call for you. Otherwise you might not have stirred.'

'Of all the cheek!' Selina exploded, only half sorry he had stooped so low. She settled back against the upholstery and closed her eyes. She could get used to such luxury very quickly. That thought naturally led to thoughts of the unknown fiancée. Jane. 'Jane what?' she asked, still keeping her eyes closed as they sped along.

'Weber.' His tone was clipped, and Selina opened her eyes and shot him a perplexed glance. His handsome face gave nothing away and she refrained from questioning him further. Jane Weber's name did not ring a bell. At least it wasn't Jane Olphin, her student! That, she could not have borne. She felt she had given him a rare glimpse of her feelings by even mentioning Jane. Now he would know how curious she was about his fiancée, and he would naturally wonder why. She wished she hadn't asked, but the question had slipped out unawares. She would need to keep a close guard on her tongue.

Elliot did not take her home, as she'd expected, or out for a drive. Their destination was a smart, intimate little restaurant on the outskirts of Croydon. The restaurant was one she hadn't seen before. Indeed, it was so discreetly tucked away that she would have passed it by.

Elliot was known to the proprietor, a tall, auto-cratic Frenchman, and Selina wondered sadly whether he'd brought Jane here. Crossly she flicked back a strand of slightly damp hair. Forget Jane, she told herself. When Elliot wants to talk about her, he will. Those in love liked nothing better than to discuss their loved one with anyone who would listen. Selina had often acted as a sort of agony aunt to colleagues in her students days, listening to tales of perfect love and romantic hopes. There was no one with whom she could discuss Elliot, not even her father or stepmother. Or sister.

Peta. He had no right to string Peta along in that way. He was promised to this Jane Weber and he ought to be faithful to her. She would tell him so when the opportunity arose, Selina decided morosely.

A menu was put into her hands, startling her. She was miles away.

'The steak here is excellent,' Elliot murmured. 'Or what about *poulet rôti*? Or . . .'

'The steak will be fine, thank you,' she said politely. She wasn't hungry. She wanted to hear about Jane. Elliot need not have bothered with a meal.

'Some wine?'

'Um? Oh, yes. Yes, thank you.' She dropped her eyes to the menu again, but saw nothing of it. She wondered what dish Jane preferred. Did *she* have the excellent steak? What did she have as a starter?

'We'll have the soup *du jour*, shall we, Selina?' Without waiting for her reply he ordered, and the waiter glided away.

Perhaps Jane liked soup, Selina mused resentfully. Perhaps Jane preferred him to order for her, as well. Evidently a woman without a mind of her own.

'You seem cross, Selina. Have I said something to annoy you?'

She shot him a resentful glance and he chuckled. 'I'm sorry I'm not Martin. However . . .' He glanced at his watch. 'We've got an hour.'

'An hour? What happens after that?' Was Jane going to put in an appearance? Selina's eyes darkened at the thought.

'Martin is going to pick you up and take you for a drive. There's a little club he knows not far from the West End. You will probably finish your evening there,' he went on conversationally, and Selina wanted to hit him.

She couldn't tell him that Martin's company would be unwelcome after his. Nor could she say how much she wanted to spend the evening with him alone. Holding her tongue was an effort, but fortunately the soup arrived and she was spared further conversation.

She took her first spoonful. 'Mm. Mushroom. My favourite,' she murmured appreciatively.

'I wanted to explain about Jane.'

The soup lost its flavour, but Selina went on with it, nevertheless. She eyed him covertly. 'Your fiancée is hardly my business, Mr Richmond,' she said crisply.

His face darkened. 'Elliot.'

'Elliot,' she amended, not wanting to quarrel with him. She liked the name. It had an authoritarian ring to it. An arrogant name to suit an arrogant man. An ordinary name like George or Keith would not have suited him.

'She's in the USA. She comes home in October.'

October. Not that long. 'Oh?' Selina said politely.

'She's a doctor. A brilliant one. We . . . we got engaged before she left. Half-engaged,' he went on, almost to himself. He pushed his soup plate away, and she felt for him. He was missing Jane so much.

'If it hurts to . . . to talk about her, don't,' Selina begged. She couldn't bear it if he poured out his troubles. She would be crying for him as well as for herself.

'You remind me of her.' He smiled, presumably to show that it was a compliment.

'Oh.' She supposed it *was* a compliment. Jane was pretty. Nevertheless, he implied that he took a passing interest in her only because she reminded him of another woman.

The steak was put before her and she stared down at it numbly. You remind me of her. Good old Selina. You are going to be agony aunt again . . .

CHAPTER EIGHT

SOMEHOW Selina got through the meal without crying. Her eyes burned with the weight of unshed tears. She didn't want to listen to stories about Jane Weber. She preferred not to know. She'd been curious before, of course, but now she knew Jane's surname and occupation and whereabouts, she didn't want to know anything else.

Once started on the subject of Jane, however, Elliot seemed unable to stop. His face gave nothing away. It did not crumple before her eyes, nor did he surreptitiously wipe away an unmanly tear. Yet she knew how deeply he cared for the woman. He must do, else why should he spend their remaining hour talking of nothing else?

They finished with cheese and biscuits and coffee. They were sitting over their coffee when Elliot glanced at his watch. 'Great heavens! I promised to be at the front entrance ten minutes ago!'

'Time passes quickly when you're having fun,' Selina said sweetly. Far from feeling sorry for Jane, as she had at the beginning, she'd now grown to hate her. If she never heard another word about the woman it would be too much. The sooner she returned and claimed the lovelorn Elliot, the better. Tears glistened in her blue eyes as Selina stole a glance at him. His face was turned from her as he called for the bill. Her fingers itched to touch him, to caress that arrogant face, to smooth away the worry lines. Idly she wondered what his hair would be like to touch. Would it be crisp and harsh against her fingers? She . . .

He turned suddenly and their eyes met. Hastily she veiled her expression. What a laugh he and Jane would have if ever he found out how much his ward sister loved him! That thought lent a coldness to her polite thanks for the splendid meal. She would have enjoyed it so much more if they'd discussed gory operations! Anything was preferable to the subject of Dr Jane Weber.

An irritated Martin Lenton was hovering in the foyer of the restaurant, and Elliot was profuse in his apologies.

'I needed to talk, and Selina is a good listener, Martin. Thank you for lending her to me,' Elliot added, and Selina went white with fury.

'I am not an umbrella or . . . or an old raincoat to be lent out!' she hissed. Because she had to keep her voice down it was difficult to put as much anger into it as she wished. 'I'm a *person*, and I don't belong to Martin for him to hire out to old friends!' she finished, her flashing eyes raking Martin as well as Elliot.

Martin looked embarrassed, but if she hoped to discomfit Elliot as well, she was out of luck. He chuckled, white teeth gleaming in his tanned face, and Selina hated Jane Weber anew.

Her eyes filled with tears and she swung abruptly away. She didn't want to spend the rest of her evening with Martin. No one could make her. The arrangements had been made without either of them bothering to consult her. Male chauvinistic piggism with a vengeance!

Selina heard them arguing behind her as she hurried out into the soft velvet night. Fortunately a taxi drew up as she began to walk, and she escaped into the darkness of its back seat. Once before she had ended an evening with Elliot by going home in a taxi. It was getting to be a habit.

Elliot wasn't far behind and she had been in her room perhaps five minutes or so when he arrived. Selina inched the door open, wishing it had a chain. In his present mood he would probably snap the chain in two with his bare hands, she thought with a little thrill of horrified excitement. She had no choice. He demanded admittance. Reluctantly she let him in, leaving the outer door ajar.

'So you can scream for help if necessary?' he asked sarcastically, and she gritted her teeth.

'Yes! I might call on Melanie Ovenden for help!' she snapped. 'She must know how to handle you.'

To her chagrin he laughed. His shoulders shook with the effort and he turned away, trying to smother the sound.

Selina had gone too far to stop now. While they were on the subject of his women she might as well give him her opinion. Determinedly she closed the door. This might take some time and she didn't want to be disturbed.

'It's time for a few home truths!' she flung at him. 'You have no right to string Melanie and my sister along! What will poor Jane think when she comes home?'

He ignored the last sentence, to her annoyance.

'Am I stringing Melanie and Peta along?' He seemed amused by her charge.

'Well, of course you are! Melanie can take care of herself, but it's Peta I'm concerned about.' She'd got her temper under control now, but it would flare up again if he kept hedging.

'Are you sure it's Peta you're thinking of?'

The question threw her, and she was about to defend herself when he went on, 'It sounds to me very like sour grapes. *You* want me, and you are jealous of your pretty, personable and charming little sister,' he went on, sounding as if he was enjoying himself.

Selina gasped. She felt her colour rising, for what he said was only too true. She *was* jealous of Peta. And Melanie. And Jane. Particularly Jane. He was hateful to throw that at her. Hateful! Jane could have him and welcome. 'I do *not* want you, Elliot Richmond! It seems as if every other nurse in the hospital has sampled your favours!' she went on recklessly, hoping to provoke him to anger. She was unsuccessful.

'Are you sure *you* wouldn't like to sample my favours, Sister Harding?' He moved nearer and, alarmed, she stepped back.

'No, I would not!' she snapped, half hoping he would take her in his arms and kiss her. Of course, she would resist but . . .

'I won't offer my favours then. Good night.' Gently he eased her away from the door and went out, still chuckling.

Selina couldn't believe it. She was so sure he intended kissing her. She was so sure she wanted

him to, as well. She hadn't stirred him to anger or
unleashed passion. Instead, she made him laugh!
That was the most galling factor of all. He had
laughed at her!

She almost tore her clothes off—the pretty suit,
her sandals and flesh-coloured tights. Angrily she
flung them down, then kicked them across the floor
to relieve her feelings. She loathed Elliot
Richmond! Each time she kicked her clothes she
pretended she was attacking him.

When her anger was spent she collapsed on top
of her bed and wept.

Selina wasn't looking forward to the weekend. She
was free from Friday lunch-time until Monday
afternoon. Virtually three days to do as she wished.
Without the one she loved by her side, the three
days of freedom meant nothing. She might just as
well work.

She worried about the ward and her patients,
too. Being a ward sister was so new to her that she
didn't want to spend three days away from her job.
Something might go wrong. They might lose a
patient, or there might be trouble. She hadn't
forgotten Mrs Gibson. At the back of her mind was
still the thought that the woman might cause
trouble. It was ridiculous and she tried to shrug the
idea away. Yet it persisted all through her
weekend.

She had arranged to spend Sunday at home with
Joan and her father. Perhaps she harboured the
faint hope that the dynamic Mr Richmond might
materialise. Hope died slowly. There were only the

three of them until early evening, when Peta walked in. If Selina expected Elliot to follow, she was disappointed.

'I've got loads of revision to do, Selina,' Peta began brightly. 'I went to your room but I met Elliot and he . . .'

'Elliot?' If Selina's voice was cold, Peta appeared not to notice.

'Yes. He and Melanie were going out. So I got them to give me a lift. I thought if you're finished, we could go back together and begin on my new textbook. Have you seen it?' Peta chattered away but Selina wasn't listening. Elliot and Melanie were going out. To that little restaurant in Croydon?

'Oh, and he asked me to give you a message.'

'Who did?' She wasn't in the mood for Peta's idle chatter.

'Elliot, of course! He said to tell you that no one is sampling. It's an odd message, but he said you would understand.'

Selina coloured. She understood only too well. Her own words thrown back at her. 'I suppose he was laughing when he said that,' she muttered, and Peta shot her a perplexed glance.

'Yes, he was. Is it a sort of "in" joke?'

'If it is, Elliot Richmond has a warped sense of humour,' Selina said bitingly.

With the wretched weekend behind her, Selina was glad to be back on duty on Monday's late shift, and arrived before the patients had finished their lunch. It was with a sense of shock that she saw Andrea Forman on the ward. For a few hours she'd forgotten that the staff nurse was beginning work this morning.

Mentally shrugging aside her dislike, she forced warmth into her voice when she greeted her new nurse. For the sake of the patients, personal feelings must be pushed to one side.

Andrea smiled pleasantly, but her light-coloured eyes were watchful. 'The PNO's secretary rang, Selina . . . I mean, Sister. You are to see Mrs Taylor at two.' She glided away and Selina thoughtfully sat down. Why should the PNO want to see her? Perhaps it had something to do with Staff Nurse Forman starting on the ward.

She found out that the interview had nothing to do with Andrea Forman. It concerned Mrs Gibson, the thyroidectomy patient who had been so reluctant to leave the hospital.

'Why on earth didn't you tell *me*?' The PNO was angry and Selina couldn't blame her. Mrs Gibson had written to the hospital administrator, complaining of her treatment at the hands of Ward Three staff. That she had waited several days made matters worse. Evidently she had been brooding on the supposed injustice of it all. Her letter, which Mrs Taylor let Selina read, poured invective upon the head of Sister Harding. If it hadn't been for Sister Harding, the ex-patient implied, her eventual discharge would have been much happier. As it was, the letter ran on, she'd been harried and almost driven from the ward in tears. The Irish student nurse who lied to her about casualties did so because she was afraid of what Sister would say if she failed.

Selina sat astonished throughout it all. The letter, several pages long, was one big lie, and she said as much.

Mrs Taylor sighed. 'I've no doubt it is, Sister, but it means an informal inquiry, nonetheless. She threatens to write to the local paper *and* the Daily Dirt and Sunday Smear.'

'Do you want me to resign, then?' Not that she was at fault, but Selina wanted to spare Mrs Taylor the embarrassment of asking for her resignation.

'Good heavens, no! Are you out of your mind, woman?' The PNO, a kindly grey-haired lady, was seldom driven to anger, but this was a day she chose to be. 'We would be playing right into this wretched woman's hands if we allowed you to resign.'

'Yes, of course.' Selina roused herself from her dejection. She would be staying on Ward Three, even if her reputation was somewhat tarnished. She left the office shortly afterwards, the PNO's words of warning ringing in her ears.

Another voice rang in her ears as she pushed open the doors of the ward. Andrea Forman's voice was raised in anger. Selina hurried into the office, the door of which was half open. Andrea was seated at the desk, with Louise Coleman standing penitently in front of her.

Andrea frowned when she saw Selina. 'It's quite all right, Sister. I can handle this for you.'

'If Nurse Coleman has committed some misdemeanour, perhaps *I* should be informed, Staff Nurse,' Selina said coldly. She was in no mood to trifle with Andrea. She had enough troubles without a staff nurse getting above herself. If a student was at fault it was something for the ward sister to deal with, or perhaps a staff nurse might take the girl to one side and gently point out her error. There were ways and means of setting the learners on the right track—and shouting at them simply would not do.

Andrea flushed but bit back whatever she had been about to say. Pupil Nurse Coleman seemed about to burst into tears, so Selina shooed her gently from the office. It was the girl's last week on the ward and there was her ward report still to be written. It would not be a very good one.

Andrea rose reluctantly from Selina's chair. 'I do feel strongly, Sister, that . . .' she began, but irritably Selina waved her to silence.

'Raising your voice to a learner, particularly one like Nurse Coleman, isn't a good way to begin,' Selina said firmly. 'The girl does her best. I know it isn't always good enough but . . .'

'We can't afford to be too soft with learners!' Andrea snapped. 'I think discipline needs tightening up. That enrolled nurse was insolent to me this morning,' she went on, her voice and face filled with bitterness.

'Nurse Baxter? I hope you will get on well together, Andrea. She's the backbone of Ward Three. I can't imagine what I would do without her.'

Andrea seemed at a loss for words, so Selina went on in a gentler tone, 'What has Nurse Coleman done, anyway?'

The staff nurse shrugged. 'She keeps bumping

into people and dropping things. I was just warning her not to be so careless, that was all.'

'She leaves this week, so that will be *one* problem less,' Selina emphasised, and Andrea coloured.

'I know you don't like me! I know you didn't want me on this ward! It should have been mine!' she protested, and flounced out, leaving Selina feeling at least ten years older. The pleasures of being a ward sister were sadly overrated!

Somehow Selina got through the week without doing Andrea Forman a serious injury, but it was a close call. All that kept her going was the thought of Pam's party. She was genuinely looking forward to it, even though she knew she was supposed to give Howard the hands-off sign as far as young Pam was concerned. On the spur of the moment she decided to invite Peta. She and Pam were bound to have something in common and they might both benefit from the meeting.

Peta accepted eagerly, and wanted to know who would be there.

'Most of Ward Three's staff, I should think. I told Andrea Forman about the party, though she wasn't on the ward when Pam was in. She might come— but I hope not.'

'Oh, her! Bossy Boots, we called her on Ward Two!'

'Yes, I was forgetting you've suffered her company on your ward,' Selina said thoughtfully. 'I try to be pleasant but I think she sees it as a weakness.'

'She does,' Peta affirmed. 'You have to stand up to her. I do.'

'That won't get you a very good ward report, pet. You have to think about your future. Once branded a . . .'

'I don't care any more. I . . . I might not finish my training.'

Peta refused to meet Selina's incredulous gaze. *Why* wasn't she continuing her training? *Why?* Was it something to do with Elliot Richmond? Selina licked her dry lips. 'Elliot has been invited. To Pam's party, I mean.'

Peta brightened. 'I'm glad. Perhaps he'll dance with me. Will there be dancing?'

'I expect so,' Selina said cautiously. 'I don't know who he will bring. Perhaps Melanie.'

'Yes, he might.' Peta's eyes were on her surgical textbook and Selina gleaned nothing from her sister's tone. Peta didn't appear to care that Elliot would have another woman in tow. It was all too perplexing, and her head began to ache.

Peta said no more about not finishing her training and Selina didn't like to pry. Perhaps at the party all would be revealed.

The Hargreaves family lived in an old Victorian house about two miles from the hospital. They occupied the ground floor flat and had the use of the garden.

The noise of the party was muted when they got there, Selina having deliberately arrived early in order to help if she could. She and Peta found themselves in a big sitting-room almost cleared of furniture. One or two chairs had been left, but beanbags and cushions were provided instead.

Derek was talking to Pam and they both came forward to greet Selina.

While Pam and Peta wandered off in the direction of the stereo unit, Selina found herself in a corner with Derek, something she had wished to avoid. He squeezed her arm. His touch gave her goose-pimples, but she tried not to flinch.

It was Derek who abruptly dropped his hand. 'Sorry. Your chief warned me off before. He said you were spoken for.'

Selina felt guilty, wondering if Derek would congratulate Martin on his non-existent engagement! 'Yes, well . . .' she began awkwardly, but Martin walked in then, closely followed by Elliot and Melanie, and a couple of nurses she knew only by sight, probably from Theatre.

She gave them all a bright smile, though her heart ached to see Elliot and Melanie standing so close together. Melanie was a pretty girl and she looked lovely tonight, her fair colouring emphasised by the lime green dress she wore. Her long hair was loose, and a series of gold chains encircled her slender waist.

Selina felt big and gauche by comparison. The vivid green dress that contrasted so well with her own colouring seemed a bit gaudy now. The neckline made her generous breasts look even bigger, she decided. She felt a frump. There was no other word for it. How could she expect Elliot to notice her when the slender Melanie Ovenden was near to hand?

Beyond murmuring a polite, 'Good evening, Sister,' Elliot paid her no attention at first, so she was able to concentrate on what Derek was saying. He introduced her to Howard Barton, a tall, bespectacled young man. Selina took an instant liking to him. Whether she could persuade Derek and his mother of Howard's suitability was another matter. She was annoyed at being put in such an awkward position. Derek was presuming a lot. Just because she was a ward sister she was expected to sort out everyone's problems. Why, she couldn't even solve her own!

'You look cross, Selina.' Elliot was by her side and she hadn't heard his approach.

'I *am* cross,' she muttered. 'People take me for granted, expect me to be a sort of . . . of agony aunt! Because I'm a ward sister, they . . .'

'Ah! Tired of being a sister already?' Elliot mocked. 'Shame on you. The ink isn't dry on your new contract, and already you're wanting a change!'

'I do not!' Selina insisted, seeing the lovely Melanie approaching. 'Your friend is coming.' She turned away, sick with jealousy. Yet if she was suffering, surely Peta must be suffering more? Idly she glanced around, but Peta's bright blue pants suit was nowhere in evidence. Then she found Martin at one elbow and Derek at the other, and she laughed. Let Elliot see how little she cared!

The party gathered momentum as the evening wore on, and by midnight everyone was dancing or laughing and drinking. Out of the corner of her eye Selina saw Nurse Baxter dancing with Elliot, and couldn't help chuckling. Elliot was well over a foot taller than the SEN, who looked rather uncomfortable tilting her head right back so she could carry on a conversation. Melanie was dancing with a stranger, and Peta was standing in a corner talking to Pam.

It must have been Elliot's sense of duty that brought him across to her. After escorting Nurse Baxter back to her husband, he made his way through the crush of bodies.

'May I have this dance?' he asked politely, and Selina went hesitantly into his arms. He may have misconstrued the hesitation, but her reluctance was for a different reason. Being in his arms would be bitter-sweet, almost unbearable.

She need not have worried. Elliot held her gently and kept their bodies a little apart, just the way he'd held Mary Baxter. He didn't *want* to hold her tightly. Perversely, Selina was cross, though she realised the injustice of her annoyance. This way was better. He wouldn't hear the pounding of her heart, feel the responsiveness of her body. She ought to be pleased that their bodies weren't touching. Yet, if only . . .

Tenderly he kissed her cheek when the music stopped, and tears sprang to her eyes. Fortunately Martin was waiting for the next dance, and Selina tightened her grip on her self-control. It was a beautiful kiss, soft and gentle as swansdown, and she wanted to run from the room and cry in a dark corner because of its poignancy.

Because the evening was cool she didn't fancy a swim later, even though she had brought her modest one-piece swimsuit. Peta was keen, though, and she and Howard assured her they would see that

Pam came to no harm. Selina told them to hurry, before Derek and his mother found out. Not being too sure how far Peta's good sense went, she followed them to the next-door garden.

The pool was small and already crowded. She noticed Elliot standing quietly by, watching. The light from the house illuminated him. He was a lonely figure. Being a consultant, he had to remain aloof to some degree, and Selina wished she could draw his arm through hers and hug him. That was love, wasn't it? A need to help the loved one, an urge to smooth his path, chase away his sorrows . . .

Derek must have heard Selina's heartfelt sigh, for his arms encircled her waist and he pulled her against him. His breath smelled strongly of alcohol, and she tried to wriggle free. She managed to do so only after stamping on his foot with her sharp-heeled sandals. With a grunt he let go, and she moved a few inches away. She didn't want to turn it into a major production. Anyway, she felt she ought to mention Howard. The pool was being cleared now, at Howard's insistence, so that Pam could have a swim, and Selina watched them from her vantage point, safe in the darkness. 'Pam is enjoying herself,' she murmured.

'What? That's Pam down there? With that blasted brainless do-gooder!' Derek swore and would have lumbered off towards the pool if Selina hadn't put out a hand to stop them.

'Let them be, Derek. Please,' she added. 'Peta, my sister, is with Pam. She won't come to any harm.'

'No, perhaps not, but Mother is so careful of Pam and . . .'

'I understand, Derek, but we can't live someone else's life. I'm over-protective of my sister, who is the same age as Pam. But Peta must make her own mistakes,' Selina added softly, thinking of Elliot.

'And I must make mine,' Derek put in, reaching for her so suddenly that she had no chance of evading him. 'Even if you *are* heavily engaged elsewhere, I intend to have a kiss,' he went on, as she began to struggle. 'Please. It's host's privilege.'

'Just one then.' She relented, but wished she hadn't as the kiss went on. He was somewhat inexpert but fancied himself as a great lover. Either that or the drink was rendering him incapable. His kiss burned her mouth and his breath was foul. Worse still, his ardour nearly bowled them both over. His groping hands were reaching for her breast when Derek slipped and almost fell. Selina pulled herself free, and ran trembling fingers through her curls as she struggled for control. That was the last time she got within grabbing distance of Derek Hargreaves!

She walked quickly towards the pool, then saw Elliot's figure detach itself from the shadows. 'Enjoy your passionate interlude, Selina?' His voice was chilly, distant, and she felt awful.

'It wasn't my fault! He . . . he took advantage of me!'

'A big girl like you shouldn't need protecting,' he said harshly. 'It seemed to me that it was Hargreaves who needed help,' he went on unpleasantly, and Selina almost took off like a rocket for Mars.

'Just you listen to me, Elliot Richmond!' she began, her breasts heaving with emotion. She wasn't allowed to continue. Swiftly he drew her back into the shadows and then his lips claimed hers. She felt herself drowning in emotion, and clung desperately to Elliot.

'Selina,' he murmured against her hair, and she moaned softly. 'This is hardly the time and place.' His voice was tinged with regret but, even so, he put her from him.

'Elliot . . .' she began, afraid he was going to leave her. But he was already gone. Her anguished eyes saw him rejoin Melanie.

Selina was no more than someone with whom he could exchange a light-hearted kiss in the darkness, and she almost cried with the pain.

CHAPTER NINE

RETURNING to work after the party was very hard. Selina was on early duty the day after and had difficulty in concentrating. She wished fervently she hadn't gone. She wished Elliot hadn't kissed her or spoken her name in that special way.

Fortunately Andrea Forman was off and Selina had Mary Baxter to lean on. Nurse Baxter, who had left the party in good time to ensure a night's sleep, kept her supplied with cups of coffee, so Selina didn't fare too badly. She told the patients all about the party to give them a new topic of conversation as a change from comparing symptoms, husbands, and so on!

Mrs Pettigrew, one of Guy Johns' patients, knew the Hargreaves family. 'Amanda, that's Pam's mother, is a distant relative of your Mr Richmond's fiancée,' she told an astonished Selina.

'I didn't know . . . I mean, Mr Richmond doesn't talk about his engagement,' Selina blundered on.

'That sort of thing gets around. She's a doctor, isn't she? Jane something-or-other,' Mrs Pettigrew went on. 'I expect Amanda will come to visit me, either today or tomorrow. Shall I ask her about Dr Jane? I haven't seen her about recently.'

'Oh, no! No, please don't. Mr Richmond wouldn't like it if . . . if he knew I was being inquisitive. Dr Jane is away. Abroad, I think,'

Selina added. Once summer was over, Jane would return. And then what?

Selina didn't think she could stand the strain of the wedding. Mr and Mrs Elliot Richmond. Once, stupidly, she had dreamed that she might be the 'Mrs' in that coupling. Foolish Sister Harding. Foolish *big* Sister Harding. Dr Jane was probably a waif-like creature similar to Melanie. Possibly Melanie reminded Elliot of his loved one, and that was why they were together so much.

The trouble caused by Mrs Gibson flared up again at the beginning of the following week. Andrea got to hear about it and took it upon herself to lecture Nurse Kelly on the importance of always being honest with patients. Selina could find no fault with the basic idea, but wished Andrea had gone about it in a more tactful manner.

Student Nurse Kelly was made of sterner stuff than poor Nurse Coleman, and she told Andrea what she thought of her. After that, the student went to her tutor at the school of nursing, then on to the union representative.

Selina didn't hear about it until the difference of opinion had been magnified a thousand-fold. Unfortunately that same day she was called upon to explain her own actions regarding Mrs Gibson to a group including the hospital administrator, the PNO and one or two of the others most closely involved.

The concensus of opinion was that Selina ought to have reported the matter to the nursing officer, who would have taken it further. As it was, the blame fell squarely upon Selina's shoulders. They had all hoped that Mrs Gibson had got over her chagrin, but letters had appeared in the local press, and there was talk of a TV personality taking up the cudgels on her behalf.

Selina could say nothing in her own defence, save that she was newly-promoted and had wanted to prove she could deal with the matter herself. She shielded Nurse Kelly as far as possible. There was no point in them both being in hot water. She tried to keep Elliot's name out of it as well, and was successful. No one thought to ask if the consultant knew about the woman's refusal to leave. They simply assumed he did not know, and Selina didn't enlighten them. She would take *all* the blame. She knew she was in the wrong, and trying to shift some of the censure on to Elliot or the student nurse wouldn't alter that fact.

It was then that the PNO brought up the question of Staff Nurse Forman and Nurse Kelly, and the furore the student had started.

'Clearly the girl has over-reacted,' Mrs Taylor began, 'but she is a union member and is free to complain about so-called victimisation if she chooses to do so.' She frowned, and Selina wondered what was coming next. No doubt she would be blamed for Nurse Kelly's quarrel with Andrea Forman!

'Staff Nurse tells me she receives no co-operation from you, Sister,' the PNO continued. That came as no surprise to Selina. 'If you had put the student straight on the matter in question, Staff Nurse feels she would not have had to get involved.'

'I can't see that she needed to be involved, Mrs

Taylor,' Selina said crisply, rallying her defences. 'A ward can have only one sister.'

'No doubt Staff Nurse is put out because she was passed over for promotion,' Mrs Taylor said dryly. 'Even so, you must try to get along better with her. For everyone's sake,' she added darkly.

A relieved Selina made her escape. At least there had been no suggestion that she should resign or be transferred. Nurses could be got rid of by transferring them to relief duties. They helped out on other wards or departments during sickness and holiday periods. There wasn't the same feeling of satisfaction, though, and Selina would have hated it and quickly resigned—that often being the object of the exercise. Her weary feet turned themselves in the direction of Ward Three—back to the battleground.

And just at that moment Peta waylaid her in the corridor, her bright chatter so much noise echoing in Selina's ears. Lacking sensitivity, she didn't realise she was unwanted until Selina snapped at her. Her mouth dropped open in astonishment, and Selina felt mean—but it couldn't be helped.

'Look, I'm sorry, pet, but right now I have all the cares of the world on my mind. Whatever you've got to say—can it wait until I'm off duty?'

'Of course, Selina,' Peta said in a small voice. 'It . . . it's nothing of interest to anyone else. I just wanted you to know that I'm definitely discontinuing training.' She hurried away before Selina had time to react.

Another bombshell! How many more could she take? Peta *was* leaving the Tettington. But why?

Surely Elliot hadn't proposed—no, he wasn't in a position to do so. Selina's head whirled and she felt faint. She certainly did not feel like tackling a whole afternoon's duty. Of course, Peta had hinted before the party that she might leave, but Selina had dismissed it as no more than a passing thought. Students often loudly declared that they were leaving but rarely meant it.

Andrea met her at the ward door, her expression flustered. 'Can you come and look at Mrs Leeding, Sister? I'm rather worried.'

Selina walked swiftly after Andrea, wondering what had gone wrong now. Andrea was always worried about Mrs Leeding, an obese lady with a poor colour. Her concern spoke well for her, Selina granted. Despite being rude and tactless, she was an excellent nurse as far as clinical matters went. She could be relied upon to carry out duties meticulously.

Mrs Leeding was lying back, one pudgy hand clutching a small framed photograph of her late husband. 'I think I'm a goner this time, dear,' she wheezed at Andrea, who patted her hand.

'Nonsense! Sister is back now. She'll know what to do.'

Sister Harding has some uses, after all, Selina mused. Mrs Leeding glanced up expectantly and Selina felt at a loss. If Staff Nurse was worried she ought to have phoned the house surgeon, not waited until Sister returned. Wondering what she could do, she took hold of Mrs Leeding's wrist and felt the pulse. It was on the slow side but her notes clearly stated that her normal pulse was slow, and Andrea could hardly have failed to read them.

'Where do you feel unwell, Mrs Leeding?' she asked.

The patient considered. 'It's nowhere in particular, Sister. Just a feeling I get. Every now and again.' Mrs Leeding looked to the nurse for confirmation, and Andrea nodded.

'Staff Nurse will sit with you for a few minutes,' Selina said briskly. 'I'll pull the curtains a little way and give you some privacy. A word with you first, Staff,' she went on, and Andrea flushed.

Andrea followed her into the day-room. If she expected to be told off over the Nurse Kelly affair she must have been relieved, for Selina spoke only of Mrs Leeding. No, Andrea admitted sullenly, she hadn't bleeped the doctor. She wanted to wait for Selina's opinion.

'Why, for heaven's sake? You're a trained nurse. I might have been another hour at that wretched meeting. No one could complain if whatever you did was for the patient's benefit.'

Andrea hung her head, and an exasperated Selina sent her to bleep the doctor while Nurse Kelly sat by Mrs Leeding. Nurse Kelly was another problem that would have to be sorted out in due course, but Selina decided she'd had enough of internal politics for one day. Perhaps everything would iron itself out without any action on her part. Sometimes doing nothing, keeping a low profile, was the best policy.

She was off the ward the following morning at a routine committee meeting. When she returned it was to find Andrea sitting in the office with Elliot bending over her, presumably offering words of comfort. Selina's thoughts went immediately to Mrs Leeding. Was the poor soul dead? Yet she had been making satisfactory, if slow, progress.

When Selina entered her office and tentatively mentioned Mrs Leeding, Andrea stared at her blankly, then shook her head. 'She's all right now. But that's a case in point—I was afraid of bleeping the doctor!'

'Why?' Elliot asked, his tone exasperated, and Selina waited expectantly, wondering what the crisis was.

'She doesn't like me! She undermines my c-confidence!' Andrea sobbed into a tissue, and a shocked Selina could hardly believe her ears. She wished she could join Andrea in a good cry—but ward sisters didn't cry. They soldiered on. Dejectedly she left the office. Let Elliot comfort Andrea.

Mrs Leeding looked brighter, she noted with relief as she went through the ward to see that everything was in order. Whatever had precipitated Andrea's outburst, it had nothing to do with a patient, for all were accounted for.

Elliot was still in the office when Selina returned. He was alone. 'I've sent Staff Nurse off. Told her to report sick. She clearly isn't fit.'

Selina quietly agreed. 'She seemed cut up about something.'

'Poor girl went to pieces. She nearly fainted in my arms,' he went on, his tone amused.

Selina held her tongue. Even so, he glanced at

her sharply as if expecting some ill-tempered remark.

'May I ask what caused the flood of tears?' she
asked instead, striving to be fair. Andrea may have
become unwell or perhaps had personal problems.

'I popped in to check some notes and she cor-
nered me. Said you sapped her confidence and she
couldn't go on. Don't let her worry you, Selina,' he
added. 'You look all in,' he went on, his eyes on her
pale face, and she gave him a wan smile.

'I've had a lot of trouble recently. Much of it
stemming from Staff Nurse Forman,' she admitted
bitterly.

'Get her moved,' he advised, and Selina eyed
him reproachfully.

'Do *you* move people who annoy you?' she
asked, remembering too late that *she* often
annoyed him and that he hadn't wanted her as his
ward sister in the first place.

His glance was quizzical. 'Sometimes. It depends
upon the people. If they're good with the patients, I
tolerate them—however much I would prefer to
have them moved,' he added, as if in warning, and
Selina went cold all over.

He could not be more explicit than that. He
tolerated her only because she was good with the
patients.

Heavy-hearted, she sat at her desk once he'd
gone. Recent events had drained her of all energy,
yet the patients needed her even if the surgeon did
not. She must shake herself out of this apathy for
their sakes.

Despite all the cares of the ward, there was

still Peta to consider. An extra burden for Sister Harding. When she knocked at Peta's door later there was no reply at first, yet Selina thought she heard movement in the room. She knocked again and called through the door.

It opened gingerly and a tousle-haired Peta surveyed her. 'I thought it was one of my set. Come in. I've started to pack.'

She certainly had. Selina raised an eyebrow. Books and clothes were scattered everywhere. Every drawer hung open, cases were stacked in every corner. Peta's record-player was on the divan bed, tights littered the floor. Automatically Selina began tidying, trying to bring some semblance of order to the room.

'Thanks, Selina!' Peta began pulling clothes out of an over-full case. 'It won't shut,' she wailed.

'Hardly surprising,' Selina murmured. 'Why are you going? Are you doing badly in the exams?'

'Of course not! I'm pretty bright if I *do* say so! I'm getting married, that's why.' Her back was turned, so she didn't see Selina's expression.

'Do I know him?' Selina's voice was wooden, and she braced herself for the worst.

'Hal Sayers. He's in my set. We went to Bath for the weekend with his mother. I told you.'

Selina almost cried with relief. All that worry about nothing! 'Must you give up your training?' she murmured, prepared to forgive Peta even that now. It was a shocking waste of tutorial time—a waste of Peta's life, too.

Peta shrugged. 'I don't want to, but Hal has got his studying to do. If I get a job with regular hours, I can help him. Earn a bit more, too.'

That was sensible. Coming from the scatty Peta, it was surprisingly so! Nevertheless, Selina left with a heavy heart. Peta might one day have been a good nurse and it was sad that she was giving up so early in her training. Selina didn't attempt to try to change the girl's mind. Stubbornness ran in the family! At least she hadn't yet given her notice. She was packing ready to move in with Hal's mother.

Selina met Elliot later that evening. He was alone but clearly heading for Melanie's room. Selina tried to keep the contempt from her voice as she told him about Peta. How could the man pretend to care for Melanie while all the time he was engaged to another woman!

'I'm sorry about Peta. It's a shocking waste—of everything,' he added. 'Do I know the man? The name has a familiar ring.'

'Peta spent a literary weekend with Hal and his mother. She mentioned it when you were at my father's house. When you and Peta were friends,' she went on, unable to stop herself.

An amused smile came to his handsome face. 'Peta and I are still friends, as far as I know. I must see what I can do to cement the friendship. However,' he glanced down at the intriguing gift-wrapped box in his hands, 'in the meantime I must leave these for Melanie.'

'Of course,' Selina said numbly. They looked like chocolates. She was particularly fond of chocolates but no one was likely to buy her any. That made her think of Martin. He hadn't been around lately. She frowned. She had got used to him, rather like a comfortable old coat that was too nice to throw away.

Idly, Elliot ran cool fingers across her brow. 'You will get wrinkles, Selina.'

She almost flinched at his touch. Although his hands were cool they felt hot to her, burning where they touched. 'I . . . I was thinking about Martin, as a matter of fact.'

Elliot seemed about to say something, then thought better of it. 'I haven't seen anything of him lately. Except in Theatre.'

'No, neither have I. Even when he's been to see some of the patients, I've missed him somehow,' she murmured.

'Could be a good thing,' he said obliquely, then swiftly dropped a kiss upon her startled, parted lips, before hurrying up the stairs.

Her heart flew upstairs with him. All thoughts of Martin had vanished.

Elliot's ward round. He was early as usual, but the ward was ready for him.

Selina watched Staff Nurse Forman glide up the ward. She appeared to move on well-oiled wheels. Fascinating. Andrea hovered in the doorway, then went out again, and Selina heard Elliot's voice. They were talking a long time and Selina tapped her foot impatiently. The sooner he started, the sooner the ward and the ladies could settle down.

When he appeared he was in a mood, and she sighed inwardly. Andrea's tear-stained face was just behind his registrar and Selina wondered what sad tale the girl had been shooting him this time.

She didn't have long to wait. They both accompanied Elliot on the round. He exuded urbane politeness but, as always, the patients sensed that he wasn't in too good a mood. This put them on edge, Selina knew. She was on edge herself, afraid lest Elliot ask her a question she could not answer.

They were at Mrs Jarmon's bed before he asked her an awkward question. Still tense, she stumbled over the answer. Then she got it wrong, for Andrea butted in with more up-to-date information regarding Mrs Jarmon's tests. Selina eyed her in astonishment, and the nurse closed her mouth and moved to the back of the entourage.

'Do try to keep up to date with the patients' notes, Sister,' Elliot said quietly, as they moved on.

'I do, Mr Richmond,' Selina stressed. 'Nurse Forman evidently has new information I wasn't aware of.'

Elliot smiled at the next patient, more relaxed now, and no more was said of the matter.

After the round there was silence while Elliot drank his coffee. Even his live-wire registrar, Ronnie, was quiet. Every now and then Andrea would smile shyly at the surgeon, annoying Selina. Then the phone went and Elliot reached across to answer it before she could. 'It's for you!' he barked, and a nervous Selina hoped it wasn't Martin Lenton.

It wasn't. He would have realised Elliot would be on his round, something Derek Hargreaves could not know. His voice carried into the office. Elliot could not hear most of the actual words, but could not fail to get the gist of it.

'When can I see you again, Selina? It's very important.'

'Mr Richmond is making a round of his patients and I'm afraid I haven't time to speak to you now,' Selina said, embarrassment turning her pink. 'Give me your number and I'll ring you at lunch-time.'

Derek began to protest, but she cut him short. Selina hung up as soon as he'd given her his office number. She hardly dared meet Elliot's gaze, and wasn't surprised when he suggested she walk a little way down the corridor with him.

'I'm sure Staff Nurse will hold the fort very efficiently,' he added smoothly, and Andrea Forman's smile was triumphant.

Inwardly seething but outwardly composed, Selina accompanied Elliot out of the ward. The registrar and house surgeon disappeared in the opposite direction, and Selina steeled herself for whatever was to come. If he dared suggest she was victimising Staff Nurse Forman, she would bite his head off, surgeon or no surgeon!

'I'm going to suggest that Staff Nurse is moved.'

Prepared to do battle, Selina felt deflated when she found the war was over. 'Moved? Where? Why?' She was anxious to get rid of the girl but that was her problem, not Elliot's.

'She's a disruptive influence on the ward. She might be better in a medical setting. Or back on Ward Two,' Elliot went on reflectively.

Selina's brain buzzed. Andrea *was* disruptive, but part of it might simply be a clash of personalities. If anyone went, maybe it should be Sister Harding. The idea depressed her. She loved Ward

Three. She couldn't leave her patients. Why should she?

'Are you still with me, Sister?' Elliot's tone was mild and Selina shot him a quick glance. There was amusement in the usually chilly silver eyes, and she took heart from it.

'I was thinking that it's only a clash of personalities. Andrea will settle down. We must do our best to get along,' she added, without much hope in her voice.

'If you and Andrea get on as well as you and I, then there will always be fireworks,' he said calmly. 'Better to make a clean break of it now. I turn off here.'

Before she could comment, he had gone, and she made her lonely way back to the ward. *There will always be fireworks. Better to make a clean break of it.* His words echoed in her mind. It was of Andrea Forman he had spoken, but the sentiments expressed could have a double meaning. He meant 'keep away from me, Sister Harding'.

Tears pricked the back of Selina's eyes, and SEN Baxter had to speak twice to her before she became aware that she was no longer alone. Elliot's voice rang in her ears still.

During her lunch-break she telephoned Derek. He was in a state because Pam and Howard were definitely going to get engaged. Selina was sharp with him. He had caused her enough trouble as it was. 'If that's what they want, you can't stop them,' she pointed out. 'Howard seemed a sensible man.'

'When can you come? Pam would like to talk to you about it. She said so. Please?' he added, and

Selina could not refuse. She arranged to meet him at their home about seven. She was free and hadn't planned anything.

On an impulse she rang Martin, whom she hadn't seen since the party and then only briefly. He wasn't in Theatre or in his office. He might be in the canteen. Selina headed that way. She still had half an hour of her lunch-break left. She needed Martin's company. She was tired of always carrying the burden.

He wasn't in the canteen, and a disappointed Selina bought a crispbread and an apple and took them out to the small but shady garden behind the main block. It was warm, and she could close her eyes and forget her troubles for a few minutes.

She found Martin where she least expected to find him—in the rose garden, sitting on the grass beside a short, plump blonde she had seen briefly before, at the Hargreaves' party. They were engrossed in each other, and she knew Martin hadn't seen her.

Selina smiled sadly. She must continue to carry her own burdens for the future. Martin Lenton had found greener pastures.

CHAPTER TEN

SELINA decided she would ask Peta to come with her when she called at the Hargreaves'. The girls had taken to each other straight away at the party and Pam needed someone of her own age at this time. Another engaged girl would be ideal.

Once the idea popped into Selina's head she had to put it into practice. There was no reply when she knocked at her sister's door and one of the other students said she'd seen Mr Richmond call for Peta earlier. Selina couldn't believe it. Elliot was trying to break up the engagement, and he wouldn't have known about it if Selina herself hadn't told him!

The student didn't know where Peta and Mr Richmond had gone, and Selina couldn't enquire from the Home Warden in case the story got around. Tales of the eminent, handsome consultant visiting a teenage student nurse would not help Peta's career if she decided to stay in nursing after all. Elliot would have had to wait in the communal lounge as it was. Male visitors weren't allowed in the junior nurses' rooms.

Selina rang home and found that Peta and Elliot were there, and she told her stepmother she would join them shortly. Hands shaking, she replaced the receiver. Why were Elliot and Peta at home? He surely hadn't thrown Dr Jane over for Peta? Was Peta's engagement merely a sham, a ploy to get

Elliot to propose? Selina had the beginnings of a headache by the time her little car drew up alongside Elliot's Rover in the driveway of her father's cottage.

Joan was at the door to meet her, her face wreathed in smiles. Selina's heart fluttered in its agitation. She could hear it, like a caged wild bird desperate to regain the freedom of the skies. She managed to return the smile for her stepmother's sake. Her poor trapped heart must learn to live with its agitation. She could do nothing for it. But if Elliot had deliberately broken up Peta's engagement, *he* would be agitated by the time she'd finished with him!

Should she tackle him about it now? She could hardly quarrel with him in front of the family, yet if she left it too long her anger would evaporate and she would forgive him. She was always forgiving him. It wasn't fair! The man got away with murder. He . . .

'Are these silent battles anything to do with me?' a familiar voice asked as Selina hesitated in the doorway. Joan had disappeared in the direction of the kitchen.

She swallowed. It was now or never. But she didn't want to quarrel with him. She loved the man, for heaven's sake! It was all Peta's fault. She was a flirt. Elliot wasn't to blame. He was only human.

'I . . . I wanted . . .' she began, but could not continue.

Elliot waited patiently. They were only inches apart. Close, but not touching. Indeed, his hands were clenched by his sides as though he wanted to touch her but would not. No doubt fighting down the urge to shake her, Selina mused bitterly, her blue eyes narrowed in pain.

She tried again, the pain of rejection more than she could bear. First Martin, now Elliot. She must be utterly unlovable to be passed over twice. 'You have no right to break up Peta's engagement!' she snarled, and Elliot grinned.

'Selina, listen to me,' he began, but a furious Selina was past listening to anyone. Elliot was a philanderer. It wasn't Peta's fault at all, she now decided. She had done her sister an injustice.

'I'm tired of listening to you! You're no better than a rake. A womaniser! Isn't Jane enough for you? I suppose it's "out of sight, out of mind."' She paused to get her breath, but before she could continue Peta came out.

'Why are you two skulking in the hall? Up to no good, I'll bet!' Peta laughed.

Selina's eyes automatically went to her sister's left hand. A diamond ring sparkled there. A fair-sized diamond, and Selina's eyes widened. No student nurse could afford such a stone. She turned her accusing gaze on Elliot, who looked perplexed.

'Isn't it wonderful! Elliot's persuaded me to stay.' Peta's voice came from far away, and Selina barely heard it, for she was drowning in the silvery-grey sea of Elliot's eyes. They were lovely eyes. Warm and compassionate. And mocking. He was laughing at her!

'You aren't going? I mean, you're staying at the Tettington?' If Selina's voice was dazed, Peta appeared not to notice.

'Mm. All thanks to darling Elliot!' Peta linked her arm in the surgeon's and beamed up at him. 'He said it was a dreadful waste of time and public money to give up now. It won't be long till the intermediate exam, and if I pass that there's no reason I shouldn't pass my Finals first go! Elliot's been helping us,' she finished proudly.

'Elliot has?' Selina longed to sit down but there wasn't a chair in the hall.

'Me and Hal.' Peta peered at her. 'You look all in. Come and sit down.' She took Selina firmly by the hand, but Elliot stopped her.

'Selina has been under a lot of strain lately, Peta. I'll run her back. Apologise to your people for me and I'll come back for you later.'

He hustled Selina out of the door, with Peta's protests following them. 'She won't want to stay by herself!' Selina added her protests to her sister's. 'She doesn't get on with our stepmother.'

'Then it's time she learned to do so.' Elliot's voice was firm, his expression brooking no interference, so Selina obediently got into his car. She was drained and much too tired to argue.

Then Peta tapped on the window. With an exasperated sigh Elliot opened it. 'What about the strike? Will you be on strike and do you think I should join it?' Her remarks were addressed to Selina, but it was Elliot who answered.

'Nurses do *not* strike, young woman!'

'Consultants work to rule!' Peta howled after them, and Selina chuckled weakly.

'She's got you there, Elliot.'

He wryly acknowledged that. 'Silly young pup.

At least she's agreed to stay at the hospital. I thought that was what you would like.'

Selina perked up. 'Did you? It . . . it was kind of you to take the . . . What strike?' Peta's words finally penetrated her weary brain.

'Something to do with that staff nurse of yours. And that student. What's her name? Irish girl.'

'Nurse Kelly,' Selina said woodenly. 'And I will be blamed for that, as well.'

He slowed the car, then pulled into the side of the road. 'As well as what?'

She wished she hadn't spoken. 'Oh, it's nothing really. A mountain growing out of a molehill.'

'I suggest you tell me about this "molehill", as you term it.' Elliot's voice was grave.

Selina didn't know where to begin. His nearness unnerved her. Then, as she stared down at her hands, she remembered Peta's diamond solitaire. 'Hal couldn't afford that!' she snapped, and Elliot looked puzzled. 'The ring, I mean,' she mumbled, less sure of herself now.

'Am I to assume that Peta is going to marry *me* now?' His tone was patient, long-suffering.

'Yes,' she murmured. 'At least, that's what I thought.'

'That enormous stone is a diagem, Selina. A synthetic look-alike. Even I couldn't afford a diamond that size! Selina, look at me.'

But she could not. Embarrassment stained her cheeks with colour. How could she have been such a fool? She put it down to her love for him. People in love did strange, unaccountable things, even people who normally possessed heaps of common sense. That was the only excuse she could find, but unfortunately she could not explain to Elliot.

'Selina?' His voice was low, coaxing, and reluctantly she raised her eyes. 'I should like to . . .' he began, and she waited expectantly. If he wanted to kiss her, why on earth didn't he get on with it?

'Sometimes I should like to shake you until your teeth rattle!' he said instead, and her heart sighed. 'Stupid woman! Can't you see further than the end of your nose?'

She touched her nose protectively. 'I may be big, but my nose isn't!' she snapped, hurt and perplexed by his remark. 'As long as Peta is staying at the Tettington, that's all that matters.'

'Is it, Selina?'

Their eyes met, but his expression was unfathomable and she looked away again. She so wanted him to kiss her—but that, apparently, wasn't on the agenda.

He started up the car again, and she stole a glance at his hands on the wheel. Square, capable hands. Surgeon's hands, healing hands. Lover's hands. But not for her. He would never be *her* lover. Dr Jane would soon be home.

Belatedly she remembered Derek. And Pam. 'I mustn't be long. I promised Derek Hargreaves I would be there at seven.'

Was it her imagination or did sparks fly from the steering wheel? 'Hargreaves!' Elliot's tone was fierce. 'What in hell's name are you doing with Hargreaves?'

'Mind your language,' she said primly, secretly pleased that he was angry. If only he was just the tiniest bit jealous! 'He wants . . .' she began, meaning to explain about Pam. Then she changed her mind. Let him stew, though why he should be concerned she could not imagine.

'Yes?' he prompted, and Selina chuckled.

'He wants to see me and I have a free evening.'

'Had,' he corrected her. 'You are fully booked now. I know a cosy little restaurant overlooking the river. We can sit and talk over our meal.'

She raised her eyebrows at that. He had a nerve! 'That would be nice,' she said coolly. 'We could spend the evening discussing Dr Jane Weber. I'm sure there's *lots* more you're longing to tell me.' She settled back in her seat, inwardly seething but managing to disguise it pretty well, she thought.

Elliot did not comment and she shot him a puzzled glance. Her message got through to him apparently, for when they stopped it was outside the Hargreaves' home. Selina, half sorry she was able to keep her promise to Derek, got out, her polite, 'Thank you, Mr Richmond,' lingering on the air as she hurried up the path. She did not look back.

After a depressing hour or so, she retraced her steps, angry that her car was at her father's home. Although still light, it was chilly, and she snuggled into her white knitted jacket, wishing she was wearing something warmer. She would have to pray for a taxi.

At the end of the road Elliot was waiting for her. He leaned nonchalantly against the side of the Rover, arms folded, silver eyes intent upon her face and chilled body.

For a moment their eyes met. To Selina, it was

like returning home after a long journey. She almost held out her hand, and was hard put to disguise the joy she felt. With a struggle she composed her features into a cool, professional smile.

Without a word he opened the car door and she got in, glad of the warmth. 'It was kind of you to wait,' she murmured as he sat down beside her and fastened his seat-belt, still without speaking.

'My pleasure.' His tone was clipped, icily polite, and she sighed.

'Did you speak?' he enquired, and Selina shook her head.

'No, I was just sighing. With the cold,' she added. 'I ought to have brought a coat.'

'Yes. It was rash of you not to dress properly,' he commented.

'That's right. Criticise me again!' she flared. How she hated the man! 'There's always some fault you can find with me. I'm only *adequate* or . . . or you weren't told of this or that! You know quite well you were told about Mrs Gibson!' Her eyes flashed blue fire at him, and his lips tightened.

'What about Mrs Gibson? I know she is causing trouble, but . . .'

'She's causing trouble for *me*!' Selina exploded. The sapphires in her eyes were dissolving, the unnatural brightness becoming tears, and she sniffed, raking in her bag for a hankie.

'My poor little lamb,' Elliot soothed, catching hold of her other hand and squeezing it gently.

Selina, astonished, forgot the hankie, and tears began to edge cautiously down her plump cheeks, as though unsure of the way. As she never cried in front of others, the tears evidently wondered if they dared fall! She wiped them away with the back of her hand, then resumed the search for a hankie or tissue. Elliot had let go of her hand after that one squeeze and she felt alone again. If she was Peta or Melanie, he might draw her head down upon his shoulder and let her cry out her anguish. Certainly he would lend her a hankie.

'You . . . you never offer *me* a hankie!' she howled, the tears starting up afresh. No longer reluctant, the tears raced down now and she licked her lips, tasting the saltiness. Tasting the bitterness of unrequited love.

'Damn you!' he exploded, reaching for her. A startled Selina found herself imprisoned in his strong arms, her head resting against his shoulder, just as she'd wished. Her heart pounded away and she gave a faint sigh. She was miserable and happy both at the same time. She had no right to usurp Jane. It was Jane's head which ought to be next to Elliot's; Jane's hair he ought to be stroking. Then all thoughts were blocked out as Elliot kissed her.

It was over too soon. A brief kiss, then his fingers were entangled in her hair as he murmured inarticulate words into the softness of her throat.

Selina opened her eyes, ashamed of the ardour with which she had returned his kiss. She was a thief, stealing what belonged to Jane. And Elliot was a cheat.

Her lips formed the words, but he was too busy to notice as he drew her closer. The next kiss lasted longer and was more satisfactory. They clung unashamedly to each other, Elliot's hands moving sensuously, leisurely over her body.

Selina found herself undoing his tie, her eager fingers getting to work on his shirt buttons, keen to be even closer to him. Flesh to flesh, heart to heart. He did not help her, gave her no encouragement. Instead his lips sought her throat, the lobes of her ears, his sharp white teeth giving her a playful nip.

'Dracula,' she murmured. Then his shirt was open and she tentatively put a hand on his chest.

'For God's sake!' He slapped down her hand, then put both of his hands on her shoulders. She could feel his fingers digging into her flesh. He was holding on for dear life, as if afraid to let go.

She felt numb—and then came fresh tears, this time of mortification. How could she behave so wantonly? What must he be thinking of her now?

Abruptly he let her go, did up his shirt buttons and then started the engine. Selina peered at him from underneath her lashes. In profile his face was stern, forbidding, the jaw even more determined. His expression was strained as he shot her a quick glance.

'I apologise, Selina,' he said formally, before they moved out into the traffic. 'It won't happen again. I don't often lose control,' he added, as the car came to a halt in the hospital car park.

'I'm glad it's a rare occurrence,' she said. 'Particularly for Jane's sake,' she finished maliciously, and hurried away, hoping no one would notice and comment upon her tear-stained face and untidy, mussed-up hair. Poor Jane, she thought bitterly. And poor Selina.

Although more important business got in the way of their discussing Mrs Gibson, Selina's remark about being blamed must have struck home, for Elliot called on the administrator the following day and took the blame for Mrs Gibson being ordered out of bed and shipped home.

Selina heard about it when the PNO summoned her. She was glad to leave the ward, even though they were busy. Andrea Forman was in a mood and no one was safe from her tongue, least of all the patients. She and Andrea had already had one set-to. Selina had been firm. It was *her* ward and the nurse must try to fit in. She neither heckled nor threatened, but the message was clear—we get on together for everyone's sake or one of us must leave.

Selina was afraid it might have to be her, but the PNO was all smiles and waved away the very idea of losing her newest ward sister.

'Nurse Forman is being moved, though,' Mrs Taylor added, almost as an afterthought, and Selina looked her surprise.

'Moving her won't solve anything, Mrs Taylor,' she said quickly. 'I'm sure—given time—Staff and I will get on better.'

'Have relations improved?' the PNO enquired, and Selina, reflecting upon the scene in her office, had to admit they had worsened.

'Then there is no alternative. Mr Richmond has requested the move.'

Selina couldn't find words for a moment. Then she said soberly, 'I should have thought he would want *me* to move. He didn't want me to have the

Sister's post in the first place.'

'Who on earth told you that?' The PNO looked astonished. Even more so when Selina politely pointed out that Mrs Taylor herself had said so.

'When you offered me the post,' she explained, 'you said that not all the panel agreed with my appointment. There was rumour circulating that . . . that Dr Lenton and I were engaged, and that I might leave,' she went on earnestly, hoping the woman would deny Elliot's involvement.

'Ah, that. Yes, I remember.' The PNO's expression was pensive for a moment, then she went on to discuss the threatened strike. Elliot's name wasn't mentioned again, which indicated that it must have been him who wanted someone else to have the Sister's post. Elliot hadn't wanted her, after all. And now it seemed he did, so she ought to be grateful.

She *was* grateful for his intervention over the Gibson affair, though he was no more to blame for the subsequent trouble than she was. The strike was a different matter and did not personally concern Elliot.

'No matter that the unfortunate Gibson affair wasn't your fault, there is still this protest,' Mrs Taylor went on, and Selina wanted to lash out in her annoyance.

'I can't see that I'm responsible for that, either.' Her tone was cold. 'It's a matter between Staff Nurse Forman and the teaching side, I should have thought.'

Mrs Taylor sighed. 'So it was to begin with. Now it has escalated. Horrible word, but it serves the purpose. An escalation from a difference of opinion to a major war.'

'A student nurse's grievance is hardly justification for a war or a strike,' Selina pointed out with some asperity. She decided, given the opportunity, that she would bang Andrea's and Nurse Kelly's heads together! It might do them both good.

'One or two irresponsible folk in the union have minor grievances about disciplinary matters, and they have been waiting for an opportunity just such as this, Sister Harding. They *want* to strike and will bring the hospital to a standstill if saner counsel does not prevail.'

Selina waited, busy with her own thoughts.

'However, these are internal politics, Sister,' Mrs Taylor went on. 'We must hope an all-out strike will be averted. I should not imagine any of the trained nurses will strike, but it has been known in other hospitals.'

A depressed Selina made her weary way back to the ward. Although the strike wasn't strictly her fault, she felt guilty because the rumblings had started on *her* ward.

By the time she reached Ward Three she was boiling. Her temper was ready to burst, and Dr Martin Lenton was the unfortunate person in her path. He rose as Selina sailed into her office. He had been sitting in her chair, and several of her folders of notes were disarranged.

That gave her an excuse to tear him off a strip, and the astonished anaesthetist stood dumbly while she told him what she thought of him.

'And I suppose *you* will be going on strike next

Tuesday!' she finished, hands on hips. She was only an inch or so shorter than Martin, so she could glare at him more easily than she could at Elliot.

'I didn't realise you cared so much,' he said mildly, when she paused for breath.

'Cared?' she echoed. 'Are you witless, man? Of course I care!'

His green eyes narrowed. His complexion was naturally ruddy, but it was redder than usual now, and he refused to meet her incredulous glance.

He didn't seem to care that the whole hospital might grind to a halt, even if it was only for half a day! She sank into the chair Martin had hastily vacated, her anger spent.

'It's all my fault,' she mumbled, hoping he would reassure her that it wasn't.

Instead he agreed that it was. She raised startled eyes to his, but he was staring fixedly at the duty-rota and seemed unaware of her regard.

'Oh!' Her voice was forlorn. It brought Martin back to an awareness of her misery, for he absently patted her shoulder. It was a fatherly gesture, for which Selina was glad. She hoped they could keep their friendship on such a level. Then she remembered the pretty blonde she had seen him with and was about to mention her, when the door was flung open.

Elliot Richmond stood there breathing fire, and Martin hastily withdrew his hand. Elliot was in a mood and Selina's heart sank. *Now* what had that Sister Harding done?

'I didn't realise she cared,' Martin muttered

brokenly as he left the office, and Selina stared after him, her face blank.

'Any problems for me?' Elliot leaned against the closed door, arms folded, eyes bleak, watchful.

She racked her brains to think of a problem. Anything to keep him near her. Anything to take his mind off whatever was annoying him. It was probably her, she brooded, as she flicked through the Kardex.

'Um, there's Mrs Little,' she ventured, reading from the Kardex. 'Had a restless night. The sedation . . .'

'They are well suited,' he broke in, coming nearer.

Her concerned gaze took in how tired he looked. The lines at the corner of his mouth were deeper than usual. 'Yes, I'm sure they are,' she agreed, not knowing what he was talking about but anxious to appease him. A good night's sleep would do him the world of good. A hot toddy, a warm bed, someone to soothe his brow. That was what he needed. Plenty of tender loving care. Then she blushed, aware that her thoughts were leading her astray. Tender loving care must come from Dr Jane Weber.

'Do you want to see Mrs Little?' she hurried on, afraid lest her thoughts should show on her open, honest face.

'If I see her now, she will imagine she has all sorts of nasties in her abdomen,' Elliot commented, placing the Kardex on the desk.

Selina opened her mouth to agree, but something in his eyes stopped her. The silver eyes weren't chilly and watchful. They were warm and tender.

Time stood still and Selina held her breath, afraid to speak lest she break the spell.

CHAPTER ELEVEN

ELLIOT SAW Mrs Little, after all, and was able to reassure her. Afterwards Selina saw him off the ward, her eyes wistful. October wasn't far away—the month of Dr Jane, as she had christened it.

The half-day strike the following Tuesday was poorly supported. Selina, who still had guilt feelings, was mightily relieved.

Andrea Forman clearly blamed Selina for the fact that she was to go on relief work for the time being. Eventually she would return to Ward Two, although Sister Cairns didn't want her back. The girl could act as holiday relief until October, anyway. Selina hoped she might decide to leave the Tettington by then.

They had a blazing row when the news was announced, and the staff nurse clearly believed that the move had been instigated by Selina. Of course, Selina could have insisted that Andrea stayed on her ward, but that was asking too much. The whole episode left a nasty taste in her mouth and she felt she had failed in some way as a Sister—failed the staff nurse *and* the hospital.

The matter did not die down as she'd hoped. She was passing the lounge door in the annexe the following morning when she heard Andrea's strident voice. She paused when she heard her name, thinking the girl was calling her, but instead she found that she was the subject of the conversation.

'Sister Harding *must* have known!' Andrea was making no effort to lower her voice. 'Staff aren't moved from a ward unless the Sister wants them moved. You can't tell me that Elliot Richmond has . . .'

Selina, sick at heart, moved quickly away. There was an old saying that listeners never heard well of themselves. How right that was! For a moment she toyed with the idea of confronting Andrea and her cronies, insisting that it wasn't her idea to move Andrea. Yet would that solve anything? Andrea had chosen to blame Selina, *wanted* to nurse a grievance against her, so that was that. People would always believe what they wanted to believe, no matter how great the evidence to the contrary.

Peta was a bringer of ill-tidings when Selina met her in the corridor just before the lunch-time change-over. Her sister came puffing up, and Selina smiled indulgently. 'Nurses never run, Nurse Harding!' she reproved, and Peta grinned.

'No, Sister. Sorry, Sister! Have you heard?' she rushed on. 'About the strike, I mean?'

Selina frowned. There was a cold feeling in the pit of her stomach. 'There weren't any nurses involved as far as I know, except two studetns.'

Peta nodded. 'One of your students, Maureen Kelly. She was off duty but she went in uniform.'

Selina shrugged. 'What she does when she's off duty isn't my concern, thank goodness!'

'No, but one of the laundry workers told her that the strike was because of something that happened

on Ward Three,' Peta hurried on, struggling to
keep pace with Selina's longer strides.

'I hope Nurse Kelly put her right. She, more than
anyone, ought to know the truth,' Selina put in
grimly.

'I defended you and so did Maureen,' Peta
assured her, and a bemused Selina waved goodbye
as they were now at the doors of the ward.

Poor Sister Harding seemed to be to blame for
everything that happened in the hospital. She
hoped the building wouldn't burn down, otherwise
she might well be accused of arson!

She was doing a spot of ward teaching that
evening when Elliot appeared in the doorway of
her office. Nurse Kelly blushed crimson as the
consultant's chilly gaze rested upon her. Selina
indicated that she could go, and the student scut-
tled out, leaving Selina and Elliot alone. It was the
nurses' supper-break and visiting hour. Generally
it was a quiet time of the evening until the visitors
started drifting away, pausing to speak to the nurse
in charge before going.

'Does that student cause you any trouble?' he
enquired, sitting on the seat Nurse Kelly had
vacated. 'Any *more* trouble, perhaps I should
say.'

'She never intended to cause trouble, Elliot. Peta
said the girl defended me when someone said I
caused the strike!'

His eyes glinted with anger. 'You appear to cause
everything!'

'I was thinking the same thing myself. Blame big
Sister Harding. *Her* shoulders are broad enough to

take the strain.' Selina's voice was tinged with bitterness.

'I hope they are,' Elliot commented, and she eyed him warily, wondering what further trouble was in store for her. 'I'm here on behalf of Martin Lenton,' he went on, and Selina waited.

Elliot rose and stood staring out into the ward. Selina saw one of the patients point towards him, and Elliot sat down again, a wry smile on his leanly handsome face. 'They will all be stampeding in! I'd better cover my face.'

As always, there was a *frisson* of awareness, of something almost tangible, a feeling she could not define. There was certainly chemistry in plenty between them. Unfortunately, on his part the emotion involved was intense dislike. Selina eyed him almost hungrily, feeling like a starving Oliver Twist type, surveying a hamper of food and being forbidden to touch it.

'Martin,' he began again. 'He's rather concerned about you. Damn the man! I can't explain for another person!' He got up again and began pacing up and down the small office, hands deep in his trouser pockets.

Faintly amused, Selina watched him. His suit was dark blue today, with a tie to match. It fitted him perfectly as always, and she supposed it must have been made especially for him.

'Do you have your suits tailor-made?' she asked with interest, as his perambulations took him nearer to her desk.

'You exasperate me!' he snapped. 'I'm trying to tell you that Martin has another woman!'

'Yes?' Selina prompted.

'What do you mean, *yes*? He was concerned about you. That's why I'm here.' He gave her an irritated look as though it was all her fault.

'If he was that concerned he should have come himself,' Selina said mildly, not the least bit interested in Martin or his new girlfriend.

'You told him you cared about him and, having a new love, the poor chap is cut up about it,' Elliot continued, as though she hadn't spoken. 'I've no doubt that you don't give a damn for his feelings,' he went on nastily. 'You've led him on, let him believe you loved him, when all the while you have been flirting. Making an exhibition of yourself with men like Hargreaves!' he charged, and Selina gasped.

Her eyes flashed and she had difficulty in controlling her temper. Loathsome man! 'A clear case of the pot calling the kettle black!' she retorted. 'What about Peta? And Melanie Ovenden? Haven't you been flirting with *them*? You haven't the right to accuse me, when *you* are the guilty one!' They glared at each other. Selina's eyes filled with tears, but she was determined they would not fall.

He saw them, nevertheless, and his flinty gaze softened. 'I understand,' he said slowly. 'About you and Martin, I mean. I don't think it matters a great deal to him. You weren't the love of his life, but Brenda is.'

'Is Brenda the chubby blonde?'

'Yes. She's new in Theatre.' He hesitated, rubbing the strong column of his neck. Selina swallowed both the tears and the desire she felt welling up.

'Are you very upset, Selina?'

She pursed her lips, trying to look severe, then hastily stared down at the surgical book open on her desk. Elliot always laughed at her when she put on her 'schoolma'am' expression. 'I'm pleased for Martin. We were . . . friends,' she explained. 'No more than that. If we had been more, it wouldn't have been *my* choice.'

'I came prepared to lend you my shoulder to cry on,' Elliot said softly, and she looked up. The grey eyes were warm, compassionate, and she summoned up a smile.

'Thank you, but it isn't necessary,' she murmured, wishing it was. She hesitated, wondering if she dared ask about Jane, but he saved her the trouble.

'Jane isn't coming back just yet, after all.'

'Oh?' Her voice held just the right amount of interest, no more than mere politeness justified.

'It will be nearer Christmas now, I should think.' Elliot's tone was bland and she gleaned nothing from it. 'Or just after Thanksgiving. The Americans hold a big celebration in November. A bit like an early Christmas.'

'How nice. She . . . Dr Weber wouldn't want to miss that.' If she truly loved Elliot she wouldn't care two hoots about Thanksgiving. She would want to be in his arms as quickly as possible. Dr Jane was unworthy of him, Selina decided, not for the first time. Fancy leaving the man to fend for himself for over a year! She could not expect him to lead a monk-like existence for all that time. Elliot was a deeply sensual man. He *needed* a woman's touch, a woman to warm him on cold nights, a soft shoulder to cry on. If he was unfaithful then Dr Jane had only herself to blame.

At that moment Selina knew she would be willing to help him to be unfaithful. If he wanted her, she would go to him, give him her all. She loved him. There was little point in saving herself for the man she would marry, if the only man she *could* marry was engaged to another woman. At that rate she would become a dried-up old maid!

She wanted Elliot, loved Elliot, desired Elliot. Out-going though she was, she couldn't tell him. If she chased him she must do so stealthily, and subterfuge wasn't in her nature. If he wanted an affair *he* must make all the moves.

Guy Johns spent some time with her the next day. Fit and bronzed from his leave, he was keen to catch up on all the gossip. He knew about the strike, but not about the dispute between Selina and Staff Nurse Forman.

'You are well rid of her, Selina,' he chuckled when she finished pouring out the whole sad story. 'Tell you what, why don't you have dinner with us one evening? Do you good after all the aggro.'

'That's very good of you, but I don't want to intrude,' she murmured, touched by the consultant's kindness.

'Nonsense! We might invite young Elliot. Make it even numbers,' he rumbled on, and Selina blanched.

'No! Not Elliot. Please.'

Guy looked his surprise. 'Still not getting on with him? He can be awkward but . . .'

'I would rather not,' Selina begged. 'He . . . isn't free to make up the numbers, to be the spare man,' she pointed out.

'Oh, you mean Jane Weber? Didn't realise anyone knew. Pity, but there's no reason you can't come alone.'

A date was tentatively fixed. Selina beamed at him, then the glow died within her as he said, 'That young Melanie Ovenden has got engaged, I see.' He took his leave, and a shaken Selina went back to her office. Melanie Ovenden was engaged! But to whom?

On Elliot's next operating day he was in a terrible mood, and naturally he blamed Selina for everything that went wrong. She had sent Miss Percy down too soon. Mrs Shaw wasn't prepped soon enough and was still wide awake and talkative when she arrived in the ante-room. And as for Mrs Devonshire . . .

'Why,' he thundered quietly, 'was she still wearing dentures? Do you not supervise your staff, Sister? Can it be that you aren't as efficient as Mr Johns would have me believe?'

Selina scowled. Elliot was standing over her as she sat at her desk. His theatre uniform suited him. Green for jealousy, she decided. 'Mr Johns has complete faith in me,' she said sweetly, the coldness of her eyes belying the tone of her voice. 'If I am not good enough for you, perhaps you should have *me* sent on holiday relief.'

'Yes. Perhaps I should, Sister,' he said curtly.

Selina was sorry she had put the idea into his head, and meekly apologised for her staff's error over Mrs Devonshire.

'You're missing the efficient Staff Nurse Forman, perhaps?' he suggested, and Selina nodded.

'Staff Nurse Michaels is very willing, but she isn't in the same league as Andrea,' she agreed. 'As I'm in charge, the fault was mine and I'll see that it doesn't happen again,' she added, mentally crossing her fingers. 'Have you seen Melanie's engagement ring?' she went on, her eyes trying to gauge his reaction.

Elliot looked blank. He obviously didn't know, and she felt awful. 'Oh, Elliot. I'm so sorry. I . . . I thought you knew.'

'No, I didn't,' he said slowly, as if dazed. 'I must see what I can do about it. Thanks, Selina.'

He hurried away and she watched his broad back until he was out of sight. He didn't know about Melanie. Now it looked as if he was going to break up her engagement!

Selina returned to her duties heavy-hearted. She must not jump to conclusions. Once before she had assumed that Elliot was trying to break Peta's engagement. She had been proved wrong, embarrassingly so. She must have proof before she threw yet another accusation at him. Yet by his own words he was damned.

On the Friday evening Selina was about to step into the bath when there was a loud knock at the door. She gathered her pink towelling bathrobe tightly around her and inched the main door open, letting the caller see just her head and shoulders.

It was Elliot, dressed for an evening out. She felt like shutting the door in his face and managed only the briefest of smiles for him. 'If you want me to give a message to Melanie, I can't,' she said firmly. 'I'm going to have a bath.'

'Are you? May I join you?' He chuckled at the expression on her face. 'Perhaps it wouldn't be wise. How long will you be?'

'Half an hour. I enjoy a long soak and there's no reason to hurry.' I don't intend to hurry on *your* account, her expression said, and Elliot laughed. He had a sexy laugh, deep and throaty, and Selina couldn't bear to hear it. She edged the door closed but he put his foot in the way.

'Will you get out!' she stormed, afraid that his attraction would prove too much for her. She was only a weak woman, after all, and Elliot Richmond was her main weakness!

'I have no intention of coming in, but I can hardly sit in the sisters' lounge,' he pointed out patiently. 'I'll pop up and see if Melanie is in, then I'll call for you in twenty minutes. We're wining and dining.'

He headed in the direction of the stairs before Selina could gather her wits. He was actually taking her out for the evening! But first he must see one of his lady-loves, she mused bitterly, banging the door closed and hurrying to the bathroom.

She was ready within the twenty minutes, even though she despised herself for hurrying. She was surprised Elliot hadn't returned, and spent some unhappy moments wondering what he was doing in Melanie's room. Despite her annoyance with him, she took pains with her appearance. The dress was fairly new, a birthday present from Joan. She wasn't entirely sure the style suited her generous curves, but she loved the dress. It was cream with faint gold stripes. The silky material clung to her body, emphasising her breasts, although the neckline was modesty itself. Low-heeled sandals completed the ensemble, together with a plain white bag and a shawl, also a gift from Joan.

Selina decided against wearing higher heels. She didn't need them, but it was partly psychology. Tall men liked looking down on petite women. Although she was far from petite, Elliot *could* look down at her if she wore low heels.

Vanity! Vanity! she chided herself as she took a final glance in the mirror. She wore little make-up as a rule, but tonight she broke her own rule. Her lovely deep blue eyes were emphasised with shadow and eye-liner, and her silky lashes were darkened with the mascara she kept for special occasions. Her full red mouth curved into a smile as she stood there. Let's see if you can keep your mind on Dr Jane tonight, Elliot Richmond!

There was no sign of the surgeon when at last Selina ventured forth, but she found him sitting in his car in the senior staff car park. His expression was far from sunny as she got in beside him. Evidently Melanie had annoyed him.

'Was Melanie in?' she enquired sweetly, as he set the big car in motion.

'Yes!' he almost snapped at her, and she simmered in silence until they reached their destination.

It was a riverside restaurant, one she had been to with a group of friends once. Selina wrapped her shawl more securely around her, for it was cooler by the river. There were tables outside on the terrace but Elliot had booked an indoor table, one giving an excellent view of the velvety evening.

'This is lovely, Elliot. I've always liked this place,' she murmured.

'Oh? Who brought you last time?' His tone was bland, and Selina fluttered her eyelashes at him and gave a secretive smile. Let him wonder. Keep him guessing, Selina, she urged herself. The silver-grey eyes narrowed when he saw that she wasn't going to tell him, and a muscle worked at the corner of his jaw.

'You've got a stubborn jaw, Elliot,' she remarked, as she studied the menu. 'Has anyone told you that?'

'Plenty of women have said that. You should try to be more original, Selina,' he said smoothly, and she flushed. Round one to her, round two to Elliot.

The food was superb, though she could not do it full justice because she was still smarting under Elliot's remark. Then there was Melanie Ovenden. Selina began on the Chicken Maryland, one of her favourite dishes. 'Is Melanie still engaged, Elliot? Or did you persuade her to break it off?'

Elliot put down his knife and fork and eyed her grimly. 'I'm hungry, Selina. And rather tired. Could I be spared the bitchy remarks?'

'Yes, of course,' she muttered, sticking her fork

savagely into the chicken. After that, they ate in silence, Selina still brooding about Melanie. If the girl fancied another man it was Elliot's hard luck. Anyway, what about Dr Jane?

The pudding was a kind of meringue with fresh fruit and cream. It was gloriously fattening and Selina enjoyed it all the more because of that. 'I shouldn't be eating this really,' she commented, after the last mouthful had gone satisfyingly down.

'No. Being big, I expect you have to watch your weight carefully,' Elliot commented dryly, and she almost spat at him.

She drank sparingly of the wine and Elliot did not drink at all. If only he would smile at her or make some cheery remark, she would be well satisfied with the evening. As it was, she faced a silent drive home. He was still in a temper and she knew it was her fault for mentioning Melanie.

Idly she glanced around, really seeing her surroundings for the first time that evening. The band was playing a slow, seductive number, one she knew well. The atmosphere was unashamedly romantic, and it hurt. Couples were leaving the terrace, coming into the warmth of the restaurant to dance, and Selina gently tapped her foot in time to the music. She wasn't much of a dancer, but she liked all kinds of music and would have been content to sit at the table until closing time. Elliot need not think he *had* to ask her to dance. She recalled vividly the brief dance they'd had at Pam's party.

She closed her eyes, sudden longing sweeping over her. When she opened them, Elliot was standing beside her, gazing down at her without warmth.

'May I have the pleasure of this dance, Miss Harding?' he asked formally, and a wistful little smile tugged at her mouth.

'Will it be a pleasure, Mr Richmond?'

'Too much of a pleasure, Miss Harding,' he assured her blandly, and she blushed. They moved on to the small, crowded dance-floor, Elliot expertly guiding her. He held her close, too close for comfort, and she feared he must hear the rapid beat of her heart. *She* could hear it.

She came up to just past Elliot's shoulder and fought down the urge to rest her weary head there, cuddle up even closer to him. Dr Jane would be doing that after Thanksgiving. Selina wondered if the woman was as tall as she was, but could hardly ask. If she'd had more to drink, the alcohol might have loosened her tongue to that extent, and she shuddered to think what Elliot's reaction would have been.

'You don't realise what you are doing to me,' he murmured against her hair, and she raised startled eyes to his, dark with passion.

Selina quivered, stirred despite herself. 'I'm only a substitute for Dr Jane,' she said quietly, hating herself for breaking the spell but feeling that she must.

'Yes, that's true,' he said equably, and she wished she'd held her tongue. To guess at the truth was one thing; to have it confirmed so baldly was quite another. He need not have agreed with her.

The dance was over and he led her back, his hand holding hers. Hastily she blinked back the tears, but he had noticed them. 'I've hurt you, Selina. I'm

sorry,' he said stiffly, his expression grim and forbidding, as though it was all *her* fault.

She essayed a smile. 'Even ward sisters have
feelings,' she pointed out gently.

'So have consultant surgeons.'

She made no comment. Every time she opened
her mouth the wrong words came out. She seemed
to have no control over them. It was as if she *wanted*
to hurt Elliot. Even her father had told her she had
a sharp tongue. Now she was the one being cut by
it, and it was a painful experience.

The drive home wasn't as silent as she'd feared.
Elliot kept up a conversation of sorts, mentioning
the food, the weather and so on. Selina did her best
to participate, grateful that he was making the
effort. Perhaps she hadn't hurt him as much as
she'd believed.

The car came to a halt, not in the hospital car
park but outside Elliot's own home. No doubt he
was going to offer her coffee. By now she was in
need of something stronger, something to give her
courage.

'I shouldn't offer you coffee, but I will,' Elliot
commented, helping her out of the car, and Selina
turned on him, her ever-sharp tongue ready to
attack. He walked away before she could begin,
however, and she hurried after him.

'There was no need to be quite so rude!' she
flared, as he opened the front door.

It was his turn to be angry and Selina backed
away from the fury in his eyes. 'You don't understand, do you? You *still* don't understand!' he
ground out. He went through to the kitchen with-

out another word, leaving her to close the door, shutting out the night.

Reluctantly she followed him into the kitchen, seating herself at the breakfast bar, aware that Jane's photograph would still be in pride of place in the sitting-room.

'At least this room isn't as dingy as the others,' he commented as he busied himself with the coffee.

She hesitated slightly before agreeing that the colour scheme in the house was on the dark side.

'It isn't mine. The house used to belong to Jane's uncle. Then he sold it to a friend of mine and I'm renting it while he's abroad,' he explained.

A friend who is abroad. Could that friend be Jane herself? In any case, the house had once belonged to a relative of hers. In a way it was *her* house. Her presence was all-pervading, and Selina began to feel uneasy, as if any moment she might pop up through a trapdoor in the floor. She supposed Jane had stayed here with Elliot. Perhaps the bedroom still held traces of her, an article of clothing, a comb, some perfume.

Selina's imagination was picturing the bedroom, and she didn't see or hear Elliot approach. She wondered what the colour scheme was like in the bedroom. The same sombre, masculine decor as the rest of the house?

'Selina, do you want coffee or not?' At last his voice penetrated the gloom of her thoughts and she flushed, hoping he couldn't read her mind.

They sat at opposite ends of the breakfast bar, as they had that evening she first heard about Jane Weber. Unhappiness settled upon Selina like a cloud. Then something made her glance up. Elliot's silver eyes were fixed intently upon her face and she found it impossible to look away.

'Selina,' he began, then stopped. She waited breathlessly. 'Nothing. Forget it,' he finished.

She gazed fixedly at her coffee, the spell broken. 'Thank you for a pleasant evening,' she murmured. 'The meal was superb.'

'It wasn't a pleasant evening, was it? There's too much chemistry between us, Selina.'

Surprised, she met his gaze again. 'That's true enough. I . . . I suppose we . . . dislike each other so much that it's impossible for us to have a proper conversation.' The dislike was all on his side. Well, mostly. Sometimes she loathed the man! Such intensity of emotion did not make for harmonious friendship.

'Yes, I suppose it *is* dislike,' he agreed equably, then chuckled at the mutinous expression on her face.

Her lower lip quivered because he'd hurt her yet again, and she pushed the coffee away, spilling a few drops on the Formica top. Being a tidy person she wiped it away with a cloth, avoiding his no-doubt censorious gaze.

'Oh, Selina. What am I to do about you?' He was beside her, prising the cloth out of her nerveless fingers. 'We always end up quarrelling. Why is that, do you think?'

His fingers tilted back her chin and she met his eyes, defiant to the last. 'You said it yourself. It's mutual dislike.'

'No, it was you who said that.' His voice was soft,

the words a faint caress. 'It isn't dislike. It's probably incompatability. We're too much alike and it's
a well-known saying that opposites attract.'

'Like you and . . . and Jane Weber, I suppose?'
she shot at him, and he nodded grimly.

'You and Jane are poles apart, Selina. She . . .'
He stopped, then enfolded her right hand in both of
his and her nerve-ends began a crazy dance. Up and
down her spine they danced, plucking her heart-
strings after they had finished. The silvery eyes
came closer and she drowned in them.

CHAPTER TWELVE

WHAT happened next was inevitable, or so it seemed later when Selina had a chance to think.

Taking her silence for acquiescence, Elliot swept her up in his arms and carried her through to the sitting-room. There, on the warm, deep-pile rug, they made love. At last Selina found out what it was like to be loved by Elliot Richmond.

Afterwards she lay in his arms, at ease with the world. A tartan rug covered them now, though she had no recollection of Elliot leaving her side to fetch it. Idly he traced an imaginary line from her nose down across her soft, responsive mouth to the cleft between her breasts.

She smiled at him, eyes tightly closed. She didn't want to open them, for she knew she would see Jane's photograph glaring down at them. Facing facts would come later. She was in no hurry to return to her lonely, mundane world. She stirred, and his arms tightened about her.

'Happy, Selina?' His voice was soft, tender. If she didn't know better she might have believed they were the caressing tones of a man who loved her.

'Mm. Very happy,' she responded, knowing it to be a lie. Oh, she was happy enough in his arms, her passion spent, her needs satisfied. It was afterwards that bothered her, the time when Elliot would remember he had a fiancée. A fiancée who trusted him, loved him, expecting him to be as faithful as she was.

It was Elliot who left the love-nest first. His lips brushed her closed eyes. A brief kiss of farewell, Selina thought bitterly. His touch released the tears which had been gathering unnoticed, and they spilled down her face. Elliot groaned, but made no move towards her. She felt the cold as his heated body left their cosy little spot. He closed the door audibly behind him, and she opened her sad eyes.

It was all over. The most wonderful moment of her life. Nothing she'd read or imagined had prepared her for that moment, for the sheer ecstasy she found in Elliot's arms. Sadly she brushed away the tears. She would remember it for the rest of her life, long after Elliot Richmond and Dr Jane Weber were married.

He drove her back to the hospital in a brooding silence. Selina would have welcomed some light conversation just to ease the tension, but presumed the surgeon was feeling pangs of guilt now. He would be worrying in case his fiancée heard about his momentary lapse.

'I apologise, Selina,' he said abruptly, as they stopped in the car park. The lights of the hospital were dimmed now as patients slept and the quiet work of healing continued.

'Why? It was what we both w-wanted,' she murmured. That was true enough. 'It was hardly rape,' she added quietly.

'No, but it was inexcusable, nevertheless. I had

no right. There's . . . Jane,' he ground out, and Selina stiffened.

'Yes, so there is.' If she had hoped he might declare his love, assure her that Jane no longer meant anything to him, that was her answer. There's Jane. When Jane returned, Elliot still intended to go ahead with the wedding. Tonight was a temporary aberration, a need for a woman. Selina had been conveniently available.

She felt cheapened, even though she ought to appreciate his honesty. He was straight with her, not offering any hope for a future together. She could not fault him in that. She'd been a one-night stand, and now it was over. Elliot was sorry about taking advantage of her, but it was just one of those things. Hard luck, Selina.

Hating him and loving him at the same moment, she hurried away, almost running in her eagerness to gain the sanctuary of her little flat. Hard luck, Selina . . . The words echoed in her mind as she went.

Selina saw no more of Elliot until his round the following week. In that time he had aged. His expression was bleak, his eyes cold. The lines on his face were deeper and he looked as if he was short of sleep. Although as immaculately dressed as ever and freshly shaved, he was a tired man, burdened with cares, or so it appeared to her.

And she was the cause of it, she felt sure. Guilt over their affair was gnawing away at him. Oh, not guilt because he had taken her highly-prized virginity. No, it was guilt because he had given in to his sexual appetite, had betrayed the woman he loved.

Ward Three was full again, and the round took longer than usual. Elliot paused longest at Mrs Eyton's bed. She was a bit chesty, though Elliot did not want to delay the operation, Selina knew. The woman was a forty-a-day smoker and was champing at the bit because Selina had forbidden her to smoke before her operation.

Mrs Eyton complained bitterly to Elliot about it, but as he was a non-smoker she got no support there.

'After you leave hospital, you must do as you please, Mrs Eyton,' he said smoothly. 'But while you are in my care, I should prefer that you did not smoke. It will retard your recovery,' he added, with the charming smile he would occasionally bestow upon patients.

The woman beamed at him and assured him that she would be good. 'Anything for you, Doctor,' she murmured, giving him a coquettish look from under her false lashes.

Selina smiled to herself. The well-known Elliot Richmond charm was still in working order, anyway!

Selina had dinner with Guy Johns and his wife that evening. To her relief she was the only guest and the meal was a cosy, informal one. They were relaxing over coffee in the couple's elegant sitting-room when Guy mentioned that Elliot was leaving for Canada in a day or so.

Canada was next to the USA. Selina's brain registered that fact, as the consultant continued, 'Some old patient of Elliot's. A Lady Something-

or-other. I forget her name. She's invited him over to thank him properly for saving her life. She's making a donation to the laser fund as well, so Elliot has to keep in with her.'

Selina made some non-committal remark, and wasn't at all surprised when Guy went on to say that Elliot was going to the USA afterwards. Of course. Naturally, since he was so near to Jane he would pop over the border to see her. Selina would have done the same in the circumstances. There would have been nothing suspicious in that if it hadn't been for the little interlude she had spent in the arms of Jane's fiancé.

That interlude had reawakened Elliot's desire to be with his loved one again. Perhaps he would confess to her, beg her forgiveness, though Selina could not imagine the arrogant surgeon begging anyone's forgiveness. His apology to her had been forced, stilted. He hadn't really meant it. No, he would tell Dr Jane the facts in his honest, forthright way, and leave her to take the matter further if she wished.

Selina's eyes sparkled for a moment as hope was rekindled. If Dr Jane was angry and unforgiving over Elliot's lapse, she might break off the engagement. Elliot would be free! It was a forlorn hope, she acknowledged. Jane would be a fool to give him up.

And even if Elliot should become free, it didn't mean he would turn to Sister Selina Harding for comfort. With both Peta and Melanie engaged, Selina was the only one available, but he would not want a serious romance with his ward sister. Elliot would play the field for a time, eventually marrying a doctor or a senior nurse or a socialite, perhaps. This noble lady Guy had mentioned, even. Selina had assumed the woman was elderly but she could well be young and beautiful and setting her cap at Elliot.

The possibilities were endless and Selina's head ached. She must try to put the delectable Elliot Richmond from her mind.

Yet even when she was in the middle of her nursing duties, she could not entirely forget Elliot. That evening she spent in his arms was unforgettable by its very nature. She went over each second of it many times, her heart thudding at the memory. If she could not have Elliot Richmond, she wanted no man. Anyone else after him would be unacceptable, a let-down, a mere shadow. Her heart belonged to the surgeon.

Selina was on the ward with a group of new nurses when she had a visitor. The girls were from the new Introductory Block and had been brought to the ward by their clinical instructor to gain some nursing experience. At the Tettington, learners began on the wards on their first day, practical work being interspersed with theoretical. This morning the girls were to help in bed-bathing. As many patients as possible went to the bathroom, the 'big bath' as it was known in hospital parlance, but three were unable to go and needed to be washed in bed. Selina was supervising two of the girls when Derek Hargreaves waved from the end of the ward to attract her attention. Selina stiffened, the lacy pill-box cap askew. Angrily she set it straight, her expression unwelcoming. Leaving SEN Baxter to keep an eye on her share of the students, she strode back to the office, still unsmiling. The man was a confounded nuisance, and if it wasn't for Pam being an ex-patient she would have told him so long before this.

'Sorry, Selina. Are you busy?' Derek smiled his boyishly engaging smile and Selina nodded curtly.

'Very busy. Was it something about Pam? I can give you a few minutes.' She indicated a chair, and a red-faced Derek sat down. Selina perched on a corner of her desk and waited. She could not forget how much trouble this young man had unwittingly caused her in the past. At one time he had appeared to fancy her, something which caused Elliot to fly into a rage. Was it a jealous rage? she wondered wistfully, her mind half on Elliot, who was due back on duty after his trip to Canada that day.

'You might at least *look* at me, Selina.' Derek's voice was hurt and she gave him a warm smile.

'I'm sorry, but I'm rather preoccupied at the moment. I have a busy ward to run.' The telephone rang then, as if to prove her point. The mornings on Women's Surgical were always busy and Derek ought to have realised she had no time to indulge in idle chit-chat.

After she had dealt with the query, Selina gave him her full attention. Pam was still determined to marry Howard and a date had been fixed. Would Selina try to persuade them to wait until Pam was older? Since they could not break the friendship, the family had accepted it but felt that marriage was out of the question. If the girl could be persuaded to wait until she was twenty-one, say, then the romance might die a natural death.

Selina was adamant that she could not and would not interfere. 'I've met Howard, tried to point out the difficulties they face. I can't do more,' she insisted.

'But Pam will listen to you!' In his agitation Derek rose and stood over her. Then, to her consternation, his arm snaked out and pulled her to one side, just out of sight of the ward. His kiss was gentle, undemanding and Selina was too startled to move.

At that moment Andrea Forman knocked on the nearly closed door and stuck her head around, her pale eyes lighting up when she saw the hated Sister Harding and a visitor obviously just coming out of an embrace. Selina went scarlet, her eyes flashing fire at Derek, who chuckled, clearly unaware of his blunder. Andrea was profuse in her apologies. She wanted a word with the clinical instructor, if Sister Harding didn't mind?

Selina was delighted to see the back of the woman so that she could tear Derek Hargreaves off a strip. He raised his hands in mock surrender, still grinning, and an irritated and outraged Selina had difficulty in being polite. When at last she had made him understand that no way was she interfering in Pam's life, it was time for the patients' elevenses and the new students were still busy with their bed-baths. She was glad the clinical instructor had more patience than she herself! No way would she be a teacher, except for the informal little study sessions she held on the ward every week.

Of course, Elliot got to hear about the Derek Hargreaves episode. The grapevine was working overtime, helped no doubt by Staff Nurse Forman. Elliot called on the ward the day before his usual round, so that he could familiarise himself with any new patients and check up on those he had operated on before his short trip abroad.

He seemed no different to Selina's concerned eyes. Weary and on edge still. Certainly he did not have the appearance of a lover who had just spent an idyllic day or so with his loved one. Maybe he hadn't seen Jane while he was in the USA. Selina had no proof either way, and she wanted to know.

'I hear Hargreaves has been wasting your valuable time,' was the first remark he made to her after he had requested the patients' notes.

'Bad news travels fast,' Selina said, a wan smile taking the edge off her clipped tones.

'There is no need to be facetious, Sister!' he snapped, and she scowled at him.

'I wonder I'm allowed to even *breathe* in your illustrious presence!' She added, 'Sir,' as an afterthought, and Elliot's cold eyes bored into her.

'If you must carry on with a countless stream of young men, I suggest you do so during your off-duty hours,' he said bitingly, and she gasped.

'What about you then? First it was Melanie Ovenden. Then Peta. "Helping her with her nursing studies," I think you called it! And we mustn't forget Jane Weber, must we?' she went on, the words of accusation pouring from her. 'Then there's Lady Whatsit!'

There was a gleam in his eyes that might have

been sardonic humour. 'I don't know any Lady Whatsit, but Melanie is my niece.'

Deflated, Selina opened and closed her mouth a couple of times, at a loss of words. 'Melanie is your *niece*?' she croaked out at last, and he nodded.

'A problem child with a capital P. She got in with some bad company. She's rather weak-willed like her father, and I've been trying to keep her from disintegrating.'

'Oh.'

'A far from easy task. I've had to squire the wretched girl about half the time,' he went on, still flicking over the Kardex.

Selina watched his long fingers as they worked through the tray, remembering their touch on her body. A strangled sound escaped her and she tried to turn it into a cough. Elliot eyed her sharply and she didn't think he was fooled. He made no comment, however, and she busied herself at the filing cabinet, taking out case notes she thought he would need.

Melanie was his niece! Selina smiled to herself at the stupid jealousy she'd suffered because of the girl. He might have told her earlier, though. 'Why didn't you tell me before?' she began, then had to answer the telephone.

He was still busy with the notes when she replaced the receiver, and did not seem inclined to answer her question. 'I'll see these three today and leave the rest for tomorrow.' He handed her the case notes.

She was about to accompany him to the bedsides when he said casually, 'Jane is coming home next week, not staying for Thanksgiving after all. I had a letter yesterday. After you, Sister.' With a pleasant smile he stood aside for her to precede him into the ward.

Dr Jane is coming home. That, Selina, is that, she thought. What slight hope there was before completely evaporated. His loved one was returning to his open arms.

Selina met the mysterious Dr Jane Weber at the beginning of the following week. She was crossing the car park on the way to her car, having been invited home for one of her stepmother's 'good square meals'.

Elliot's car was parked in the senior staff car park, part of which she had to cross before coming to her own. He was helping a tall, slender brunette from the luxurious Rover. A brunette whose laughter cut into Selina. The merry, tinkling laugh of one who was truly happy. And why shouldn't the woman be happy? She was with the man she loved.

Elliot saw Selina and beckoned her over. Heavy-hearted, but with a brilliant smile fixed to her face, she walked slowly over to them. He made the introductions and Dr Jane gave her a friendly smile. There was no jealousy in her expression, no watchfulness in her eyes. Why should there be? As far as she knew, Selina Harding was simply Elliot's ward sister. Nothing more than that.

'Jane worked here years ago and I'm showing her around the wards.' Elliot's face was one big smile, all weariness gone from it, and Selina's heart ached. Oh, how it ached.

But because she loved him she wanted him to be happy, so she swallowed her jealousy and the three of them exchanged a few pleasantries before Selina moved away. Her jaw ached from the effort of smiling, but she couldn't relax and give in to her sorrow until she was safely out of the car park and away from prying eyes.

Elliot's round on the Wednesday went off smoothly. He was in excellent spirits and even cracked a joke with his registrar. It was a good joke and Selina laughed as much as the others, though she wanted to cry.

He called on Ward Three later that day, when Selina was in the sluice, of all places. The ward junior seemed unable to understand that when a patient asked for a bedpan, she wanted it there and then, not ten minutes later when nurse happened to have the time. Selina's keen eyes had spotted a patient in obvious distress and she had hurried to the sluice to make sure that the bedpan arrived in time.

After the patient's needs were attended to, she beckoned the nurse into the sluice to help tidy the place up a bit. It wasn't where one would expect to find a ward sister, and Elliot looked amazed.

'Please, Sister . . .' the nurse began, then squealed in terror at sight of a *consultant* in the sluice. Selina whirled round, wondering what on earth was the matter. But instead of allowing Selina to return to the office, Elliot asked the junior to leave, and she did so, eyes wide.

'Wouldn't the office be a more appropriate place, Elliot?' Selina said frostily. 'The girl was helping me to tidy.'

'I'm sure you can manage to tidy the sluice without any help, Sister,' Elliot said affably. 'I've always said you were adequate.'

Incensed, Selina grabbed a bedpan, fortunately clean and dry, and hurled it at him. She could take no more. He caught it deftly and replaced it on the rack while Selina fought for control.

'I'm sorry, Mr Richmond,' she said, the apology almost sticking in her throat. 'Not the sort of behaviour one expects from a ward sister,' she went on, her face flushed.

'True, but there *are* extenuating circumstances,' he allowed. 'One mustn't be too harsh with you. This *is* your first offence.'

'It may not be my last,' she retorted. 'Perhaps you should try getting rid of me again. I might throw a used bedpan next time!'

'Have I tried to get rid of you? Warfarin in your coffee?'

'You never wanted me here in the first place! There is no point in beating about the bush, Elliot. Mrs Taylor told me one or more members of the interviewing panel didn't want to promote me!' He could at least admit his guilt.

'One or two weren't keen, solely because a rumour had got about that you were having a torrid affair with Martin Lenton,' Elliot said grimly. 'However, I wasn't among that number. I knew you would make an excellent Sister.' He hesitated while she began to apologise yet again.

'However . . . I didn't want you to be promoted because it meant I would see too much of you.'

'I . . . I don't understand,' she whispered, as he

moved purposefully towards her.

'Perhaps this will convince you.' Selina found herself in his arms, her back pressed against the bench on which they tested the urine! His mouth blocked out the sight and smell of their surroundings and she responded eagerly.

He released her after a long moment, then raked his fingers through his hair. 'You're bad for my blood pressure, Sister Harding!' he chuckled, and Selina smiled.

Her throat felt tight and, try as she might, she could not swallow. No doubt she had a cold coming. Standing in the draughty sluice wouldn't do her much good, either. She went to brush past him but he held on to her hand, twisting it so that his thumb could caress her pulse. 'Not so fast, Sister Harding. This isn't the most romantic of venues, but will you marry me?'

She couldn't believe her ears. 'You're going to marry Jane!' she exclaimed, eyes narrowed in disbelief. 'I don't want you, anyway,' she added, eager to pay him back a little for the hurt he had inflicted on her.

'Not want me?' He looked astounded. Then his full lower lip began to tremble and he turned from her.

She'd hurt him! 'Oh, Elliot! My darling! I didn't mean it. I didn't! Don't . . . don't upset yourself.' She clung to his back, aghast at the wound she had inflicted. That hot temper of hers would get her into serious trouble one day, she knew it.

Elliot was shaking, and his strong hands held on to hers as they encircled his waist. Then the muffled sound became a chuckle, and Selina's eyes flashed dangerously. He was playing cat and mouse with her! He wasn't upset at all!

She dragged herself free. 'Elliot Richmond, just you listen to me!' She wagged a finger at him, and he laughed all the more.

'We're going to have an eventful marriage, my love,' he said, the look in his eyes warming her even in the chilly sluice.

'What about Jane? Your fiancée? She . . . she's come a long way to marry you,' she whispered, afraid even now that he might change his mind.

'I had to see Jane again, explain that I no longer wanted to marry her. I worried about it. I was afraid to hurt her. And afraid to hurt you, though I managed *that* often enough!' he went on. 'I still love Jane in a way, but as a dear friend. She's had a change of heart, too, and was upset at the thought of hurting me!'

Selina smiled tremulously, her heart warming to Dr Jane Weber. She hoped the woman would be as happy as she was going to be with her rude, arrogant, quick-tempered surgeon.

Later, much later, and in a more romantic setting than the sluice, Elliot apologised for the way he'd treated her. 'I hated to insult you, but I felt guilty because I wanted you, loved you . . .' he murmured against her hair, and Selina sighed.

She snuggled up to him. They were back on the soft rug in Elliot's sitting-room. Jane's photograph had been removed and Selina no longer felt jealous of her. At last the surgeon had called for Sister Harding.

Mills & Boon

4 Doctor Nurse Romances
FREE

Coping with the daily tragedies and ordeals of a busy hospital, and sharing the satisfaction of a difficult job well done, people find themselves unexpectedly drawn together. Mills & Boon Doctor Nurse Romances capture perfectly the excitement, the intrigue and the emotions of modern medicine, that so often lead to overwhelming and blissful love. By becoming a regular reader of Mills & Boon Doctor Nurse Romances you can enjoy SIX superb new titles every two months plus a whole range of special benefits: your very own personal membership card, a free newsletter packed with recipes, competitions, bargain book offers, plus big cash savings.

**AND an Introductory FREE GIFT for YOU.
Turn over the page for details.**

Fill in and send this coupon back today and we'll send you
4 Introductory
Doctor Nurse Romances yours to keep
FREE

At the same time we will reserve a subscription to Mills & Boon Doctor Nurse Romances for you. Every two months you will receive the latest 6 new titles, delivered direct to your door. You don't pay extra for delivery. Postage and packing is always completely Free. There is no obligation or commitment – you receive books only for as long as you want to.

It's easy! Fill in the coupon below and return it to
MILLS & BOON READER SERVICE, FREEPOST, P.O. BOX 236, CROYDON, SURREY CR9 9EL.

Please note: **READERS IN SOUTH AFRICA** write to
Mills & Boon Ltd., Postbag X3010, Randburg 2125, S. Africa.

- -